OPERATION BAZOOKA

The True Story Behind the Hunt for the Most Dreaded UP Gangster

RAJESH PANDEY, IPS
RAKESH GOSWAMI

BOLD

An imprint of
Srishti Publishers & Distributors

Srishti Publishers & Distributors
A unit of AJR Publishing LLP
212A, Peacock Lane
Shahpur Jat, New Delhi - 110 049

editorial@srishtipublishers.com

First published by Bold,
an imprint of Srishti Publishers & Distributors in 2023

10 9 8 7 6 5 4 3 2 1

This is a work of non-fiction, based on the author's thorough research and experience. Some events have been fictionalised for dramatic effect. While due care has been taken to verify all information at press time, any inadvertent miss brought to notice shall be updated in the subsequent editions.

Printed and bound in India

Advance Praise

"A gritty, nail biting cop drama that will keep you on the edge of your seat!"

- Anirban Bhattacharyya
Bestselling Author
Creator-Producer of Savdhaan India

"Well written! This thrilling true account tale is not to be missed."

– Aloke Lal
Former Director General Of Police
Bestselling Author

Dedicated to Late Shri Kalyan Singh,
the former Chief Minister of Uttar Pradesh,
who had the gumption to set up
a Special Task Force to rid the state of a gangster.

Contents

Note from the author

I would like to express my sincere gratitude to the then Chief Minister of Uttar Pradesh, Late Shri Kalyan Singh ji for creating an environment that empowered me and my fellow officers to serve and protect the people of this great state. He was the decision maker behind the establishment of a unique, special and first of its kind unit in the nation called Special Task Force (STF). In itself, that was a gutsy move against the deeply rooted world of organized crime and mafia in the heartland of northern India in the '90s.

My heartfelt regards to distinguished officer Shri Ajay Raj Sharma, then ADG (Law & Order) who was foundational in ideating the concept of STF. His unwavering support, guidance and encouragement is what has strengthened the glory to the Uttar Pradesh police force in the period when crime was at its peak.

I humbly extend my deepest respect towards my mentor and my guru Shri Arun Kumar (Retd. DG RPF), who was one of the most dynamic, agile and firm decision makers I have ever met in my career spanning through decades. His combative instinct, his dedication and will to pursue tasks to completion inspire me till date. He not only encouraged us, but inculcated values like fearlessness, disciple and professional excellence.

My regards further extend to my seniors Shri Rajnikant Mishra (Retd. DG BSF), Shri Subesh Kumar Singh (Retd. DG) who enriched my experience and the force with their revolutionary and innovative approach, that propelled the force on the trajectory of progress and glory. I also wish to thank my juniors who worked with me as a team throughout my career.

I owe my journey and its success to my companion, best friend and better half, my wife Meenu Pandey for her unconditional affection, understanding, support and above all, her courage, that is actually the root of my professional existence. That enabled me to pursue my passion of serving the nation with confidence and bravery.

My sincere respect and devotion to my parents Late Shri Chandra Prakash Pandey and Late Mrs. Ram Kumari Pandey for nurturing me with the right values and ethics, that kept me going in the right direction in life. My source of confidence, my younger siblings, my brother Shri Ajay Kumar Pandey (IFS), sisters Mrs. Vandana Dwivedi and Mrs. Poonam Mishra. I would like to express my love for my dearest daughter Kriti and son Aashay, who were too young to go through many hardships due to the nature of my work.

Lastly, I would like to thank Shri Rakesh Goswami, my co-author, whom I know since ages. The memory of the day is still fresh when I first met him as a budding correspondent. His pursuance of truth, knowledge and his undying curiosity has taken him to the successful place which he truly deserves. I feel extremely elated to have witnessed his wonderful journey through years.

Your support has been a source of strength and inspiration for me. Thank you all for the contribution in my life and career that brought me where I am today.

Rajesh Pandey

A note of thanks

There's a reason why my first book is on crime.

Crime reporting has always fascinated me – from the time I set foot in the newsroom of *Hindustan Times* in Lucknow in July 1997 as a trainee sub editor, to my last journalistic assignment at *Hindustan Times* in Jaipur, which got over in October 2020. As a freelance writer, I was contributing to *The Times of India* and *The Pioneer*, besides *Hindustan Times.* The newspapers had allowed me access to their newsrooms to file my stories. During this time, I would often overhear conversations of city reporters related to politics, crime and other stories that they were doing. Shriprakash was one name that often featured in those conversations, because this was the time when the gangster's reign of terror was looming large over Lucknow. The gangster was eliminated before I took up journalism as a career. But Shriprakash had, unwittingly, spawned many other gangsters who hankered after the space that the gangster had ceded in the world of crime, and his name kept cropping up in newsroom discussions during my training period. Bishwadeep Ghosh, the crime reporter at *Hindustan Times*, Lucknow, and his aide-de-camp Bhupendra Pandey, had reported on Shriprakash's escapades extensively and were good friends with Rajesh Pandey, the author of this book.

After my training period got over and Bhupendra Pandey took over the reins of crime reporting from Bishwadeep Ghosh, sometimes in the year 2000, I would volunteer to take up crime stories to edit. The STF had got its hand on the magic of phone tapping and Rajesh Pandey would often spend nights on end to eavesdrop on phone conversations of criminals to devise strategies to nab them. While on his nocturnal shifts of listening to phone conversations, Rajesh Pandey would drop into newsrooms. It was during one such visit to HT when I met him for the first time. Whenever possible, I would tag along with Bhupendra to Rajesh Pandey's office or to the office of the SSP, called the command in crime reporters' parlance. After a few years of working on the desk, my editor Sunita Aron shifted me to reporting, but there was no way I could be given the crime beat because Bhupendra was ensconced in that beat. I got the health beat. After finishing filing my stories, I loved to sit with Bhupendra to see him file crime stories. Such was my fascination with crime!

In 2005, I shifted to broadcast journalism and joined *Channel 7*, a national Hindi news channel from the stables of the Dainik Jagran group, as its Rajasthan correspondent. (The channel was later rechristened as *IBN7* and is now called *News18 India.*) It was on television that I began reporting on crime. Harish Chandra Singh, the chief reporter of *Rajasthan Patrika*, was a veteran crime reporter in Jaipur. I took his help to dig in my heels into the world of crime reporting and was soon rushing to crime spots and doing piece-to-camera outside police stations. I quit the channel in April 2008 and joined *Times Now* at a time when Jaipur was rocked by a terror attack. My first story for the English news channel was a crime story – the Rajasthan Police got the sketches of the suspects of the terror blasts wrong. Two of the biggest stories that I reported on for Times Now were also crime stories – nurse Bhanwari Devi kidnapping and murder case, and Asaram rape case. After nine years of television journalism, I returned to the print and joined *Hindustan Times*, Jaipur, as Chief of Bureau, in charge of editorial operations in Rajasthan. Here, I led a team of reporters and was responsible for keeping the newspaper ahead of the competition in terms of news coverage. Reporters in my team, who handled the crime beat at various times - Deep Mukherjee, Salik Ahmed, Jaykishan Sharma - would vouch for my focus on crime reports. Incidentally, some big hate crimes were reported during this time. Lynching of Pehlu Khan on the Jaipur-Delhi highway and of Rakbar Khan in Alwar's Lalawandi forests, and Muslim labourer Mohammed Afrazul hacked with an axe and burnt alive in Rajsamand town by Shambhu Lal Regar.

Even though I kept in touch with Bhupendra Pandey, now the editor of *Indian Express* in Lucknow, I lost touch with Rajesh Pandey. And then the Covid-19 pandemic happened. Rajesh Pandey was DIG of Bareilly Range when the first lockdown to limit the spread of Covid-19 was announced. People were confined to their houses and didn't have much to do. Rajesh Pandey started a YouTube channel to beat this monotony and began talking about his career. I heard some of the episodes and called him. Thankfully, his phone number had not changed!

The idea for this book was born during that conversation. I decided that my first book had to be a crime story and it had to be the story of Shriprakash Shukla, the most dreaded gangster of Uttar Pradesh.

I began writing this book in June 2020 and had the first draft ready in 16 days. The final draft took a few months from there because I tested positive for Covid-19 - twice - and quit journalism to take the plunge into academics in November 2020. The final draft was ready in December 2020. Now the most difficult part began – scouting for a publisher. Many commissioning editors, who were friends on social media, had shown interest when I discussed the book while I was writing it, but when the formal proposal was sent to them, they opted out. The book lay in cold storage for some time until my friend and Indian Police Service officer Ajay Pal Lamba's book, titled *Gunning for the Godman*, was released in September 2020. He introduced me to Suhail Mathur of The Book Bakers literary agency. Suhail's excitement about the book gave me hope and finally Srishti Publishers came on board to publish the book.

I would like to express my gratitude to Rajesh Pandey for allowing me to be his co-author, to Bhupendra Pandey for introducing me to this wonderful human being and an excellent police officer, to Harish Chandra Singh for helping me take baby steps into crime reporting, to Ajay Pal Lamba for leading me to Suhail Mathur, to The Book Bakers for helming the book, and to publisher Arup Bose and Stuti, who took care of the editorial aspect of the manuscript, to Srishti Publishers & Distributors for taking on this project. I am also thankful to my friends Tarun Dutt, for being there whenever I felt diffident about the book, and Ritesh Sharma, for being my first reader and offering very valuable suggestions to improve the manuscript.

I take this opportunity to express my respect to my parents, Shri Kedar Prasad Goswami and Smt. Sheela Goswami, for raising me the way they have.

And finally, to my companion, Renu, and daughters Khushee and Ila, for enduring with my long writing hours during the first draft. Because of office work, I got time to write the book only at night and would continue well into the early hours. I am indebted to Renu, my wife for 23 years, for being the strongest pillar of strength and for keeping me sane and motivated.

I hope that readers will like this book. Bouquets and brickbats can be sent to rakeshgoswami@gmail.com

Rakesh Goswami

Prologue

31 March 1997

It was a bright morning in early summer at Lucknow. That year, the transition from spring to summer didn't linger long like other years, making people shed their woollens and get into their summer attire soon after. The season hatched a conspiracy to deprive people of the pleasant mornings and chilly nights. Along with the heat, in that year particularly, humidity became a constant companion. Although it was just half past nine in the morning, the sweltering heat of the sun sucked up the vitality of the city. The birds lacked vigour and chirped less. The scorched leaves of almost all trees drooped and were seemingly pale. People on the roads dragged themselves to work. Beads of sweat lined their foreheads and soft drinks stands mushroomed at every nook and corner. Amidst this gloom of fatigue, Spring Dale School in the trans-Gomti area of Indira Nagar was bursting with life and activities.

It was the day of results at the kindergarten school. Children, clutching the fingers of their parents, were coming to school to collect their report cards. The road outside the school was lined with vehicles. Most of the parents accompanying them were quite young. Some children were accompanied even by their grandparents. They were trickling in and out of the small building. Laughter and giggles filled the air. A few toddlers were playing in the park in the school premises. After all, they were meeting each other after a month post their previous academic session. Since it was their result day, they were not wearing their regular school uniforms. Instead, they wore bright and colourful clothes, which made them look like little bundles of joy. Their carefree smiles and fits of laughter were testimony of their innocence.

Needless to say, trauma had not touched them...*yet!* A little boy in red was pushing the swing for his friend. It was a girl with light brown curls, wearing a yellow dress with black polka dots. Her curious eyes were looking all around as she went up, imagining the swing to be an aeroplane. From the school building emerged an unsmiling couple with their baby boy pressed between them. The mother turned towards the child and said something sternly. The poor boy's eyes welled up immediately and he was on the verge of tears. Somewhere, some child was wailing hysterically.

A middle-aged man wearing a white kurta-pajama was accompanying a woman and a child. The man had a slight stubble, not pruned like those that men wear these days. It was rather an ill-maintained, unkempt beard that had sprouted like burnt ends of crops in a field after a harvest. He was wearing a pair of brown sandals, worn out around the edges. His vigilant eyes were constantly drifting everywhere, as if he could sense possible danger. The woman seemed to be blissfully unaware of the man's demeanour. She was clad in a pink saree that was otherwise plain barring the thin border that replicated plant motifs. The child was holding on to his mother's *pallu*, eyeing the group of toddlers playing in the park. The woman saw that and tried to coax him to go and join his friends in the park, but the child refused. The three slowly stepped outside the school gate and were waiting for their car. The man started searching his pocket for something, looked back, found what he was looking for, and went a few steps back to pick it up.

Ratatatatatatatata...

Bang...bang...bang...

The rattle of Sten guns, or carbine as called in police parlance, and sound of pistols pierced through the cacophony of the school noises, deafening everyone present there.

The man in the kurta-pajama fell on the ground with a thud and lay motionless on his stomach.

A momentary veil of stupefied silence shrouded the school.

Chapter 1
The Most Feared

It took everyone a few seconds to realize what had transpired. Upon realizing that the sounds were of guns, parents and guardians, along with their little ones, started running helter-skelter. The blazing guns made their blood run cold. Parents, who were closer to the victim, tried in vain to obstruct their children's gaze from the gory sight, as they ran to find a safer place. People who were away from the dead man thought it to be some kind of a terrorist attack. Trembling with horror, they cowered into the classrooms. The woman and the kid, who were with the man, had narrowly escaped death. If the man would have not moved a few steps away from them to recover what was missing from his pocket, the bullets no doubt would have hit both of them too. The woman picked up the child and both ran for cover. The kids, who were walking out, ran back in. The parents hid behind the school boundary wall.

The killers came on motorbikes and had shot the man while riding them. Three men, all wearing black kurta-pajamas, got off the bikes. A short guy holding two pistols, a strapping man of 5 feet 10 inches and a stout man with a heavy beard emerged. The tall and stout men were both carrying Sten guns. There was no resistance to the killers. After checking on the dead man lying covered in blood, his white kurta soaking in a crimson hue, the assailants began to walk away. They would have walked barely ten steps when they discussed something in hushed voices and returned.

One of the assailants kicked the dead and tried to turn over the man with his leg. The other two lifted the lifeless man by his hands. As he was pulled up a few inches above the ground, his face now towards the sky, the first attacker, who had pistols in both hands, shot each eye five times. Engulfed in madness, the assailant shouted "*Sala ghoorta bahut tha* (He used to stare a lot)."

"*Khatam ho gaya sala* (He is dead)," shouted the stout one.

"*Gandi nazaar, ganda kaam... Isko to marna hi tha* (Dirty gaze, dirty work... He was bound to die)," the short killer hissed.

He had changed the magazine of the carbine by then. Glancing angrily at the languid eyes, he again pulled the trigger of the gun. He fired the entire magazine in the chest of the bloodied man. The man with two pistols hollered to his aides, "*Heart kidhar hai* (Which side is the heart?)," and without waiting for the other two to answer, shot five bullets on each side of the chest. The three men made sure that the man on the road was dead.

"*Jab tak mar na jaye yahan se hatna nahi hai* (Let's not leave this place until he is dead)," one of them shouted as he shoved the nozzle of the semi-automatic weapon into the man's mouth and emptied the magazine.

"*Ye mar gaya hai ab* (He is dead now)," the tall killer mocked.

The body was pierced. Blood leapt out of the skull, the eyes and the chest. The three men walked to their motorbikes and escaped fearlessly.

It was barbaric. The kids were in shock for many days and traumatized for life after witnessing this ghastly murder in broad daylight.

The body was beyond recognition. When the police arrived, they found an identification card from the pocket of the dead. It said Virendra Pratap Shahi.

6 | THE MOST FEARED

Virendra Pratap Shahi and Hari Shankar Tiwari were active student leaders during the 1970s at Gorakhpur University. It was a time when mafiaraj started to show its ugly teeth in Gorakhpur. A vicious rivalry broke out between the Thakurs and the Brahmins, both fighting for supremacy. Tiwari became the figurehead of the Brahmins, while Shahi took charge of the Thakurs. Shahi and Shankar's enmity became part of the folklore.

Post their university days, after serving as students' leaders, both went on to become MLAs several times. Gorakhpur, at that time, was the hub of railway activities because of the headquarters of North-Eastern Railway. Their rivalry was centred around railway contracts. Tiwari had been an MLA from Chillupar constituency several times, and Shahi represented Luxmipur constituency of neighbouring Maharajganj district. During this time, Shahi gained the reputation of Robin Hood for his people.

Both their gangs constantly killed each other for supremacy, which disturbed the social fabric of that region. There had been so many murders between the two gangs that Gorakhpur had come to be known as the crime capital of India in the 1980s. As a matter of fact, the then Uttar Pradesh government headed by Chief Minister Vir Bahadur Singh, who also belonged to Gorakhpur, brought The Uttar Pradesh Gangsters and Anti-Social Activities (Prevention) Act, 1986, to rein in the two. Earlier too, there had been a murderous attack on Shahi near Chandralok Lodge in Gorakhpur on 22 October 1996. The attack had been swift and brutal, but Shahi was lucky - he survived. Shahi's gunner lost his life. Naturally, the first suspect for Shahi's killing was his rival, Hari Shankar Tiwari. There had been two bids on Shahi's life in Gorakhpur before the Spring Dale School shootout at Indira Nagar.

News of Shahi's killing spread like wildfire. It took the police force a few minutes to arrive on the spot. They seemed flabbergasted at the bestiality of the killing. Every inch of the body was pierced by bullets. SSP Lucknow Rajnikant Mishra reached the spot along with other officers of trans-Gomti police district. The constables were picking empties of the bullets. Police officers tried to speak to the eyewitnesses, but everyone was in shock and refused to share anything with the police. The parents at the school had already taught their children to remain tight-lipped. The poor kids didn't know what to do and they were too frazzled and fragile to let a policeperson come near them. One of the constables tried to lure a child with toffees but all that the child could manage to utter was "maa" before breaking into fits of tears. An ambulance arrived at the spot soon after and the body was sent for autopsy.

That day, an extra police force was deployed at the mortuary. Shahi's family, along with a large number of his supporters, came to the mortuary. Women and men were all wearing white to mourn the passing away of their Robin Hood. Shahi family members refused to believe that he was no more. They were taken to a room to identify the objects retrieved from the murdered man. As soon as Shahi's aunt, who had raised him, saw the broken watch that she had once gifted to Shahi, she broke down. Other family members identified other objects and it was confirmed that the murdered man was indeed Shahi. Meanwhile, the preliminary autopsy report came. The doctors found innumerous entry and exit wounds on the body during the postmortem. Hundred and twelve bullets had ploughed Shahi's body.

Police officers were trying to find out who could be behind this sensational killing. Relatives herded outside the door of the room to hear the outcome of the identification process. Some of the distant relatives started gossiping and guessing who could have the audacity to kill Shahi, that too in this atrocious manner. A police officer heard one of the several relatives mention the name of someone named Shriprakash Shukla in his ear. The relative told the police that Shukla had been contacting Shahi for six months and was threatening to murder him. The relative quickly fled the location after sharing this information. Shriprakash Shukla was a new name in the Lucknow crime circle, so the police were reluctant to believe that a dilettante could have pulled off such a daring killing, that too with such ruthlessness.

It was established later that barbarism was Shriprakash Shukla's style. Th school dropout from Gorakhpur in eastern Uttar Pradesh emerged as the most feared gangster in the Hindi heartland in the late 1990s. His father, post retirement as an

Indian Air Force officer, was a government contractor. During an altercation with a local rival, Rakesh Tiwari, Shriprakash had mistakenly shot him dead. Although Shriprakash was guilty, this incident was a stepping stone for him to enter the crime world. After the incident, Shukla was sent packing to Bangkok by an influential politician in Gorakhpur, who had assured to shield the family.

When Shukla returned to India, he started with grabbing railway contracts in Gorakhpur, the headquarters of North-Eastern Railway, and graduated to Lucknow to a point when he planned to kill people close to the then Chief Minister.

The man started his journey at the young age of twenty-one and was killed in a police encounter at twenty-six. But in these five years, his name evoked nothing but terror because of his modus operandi. He was the first criminal to use an AK-47 rifle and would fire fifty to sixty bullets to kill one person. He was intrepid - the location and target didn't matter; he would strike at will. After establishing his name for the daring killings, he took to kidnapping for extortion. Shukla would demand crores as ransom, which was a huge amount in the 1990s.

The story of Shriprakash Shukla was exciting for the modus operandi and for the chase. The police didn't even have his photograph when his name emerged in two sensational murders in the state capital in early 1997. Shahi's murder was the second.

The Special Task Force (STF), one of India's most elite police forces, was formed during the reign of Shriprakash Shukla. I, Rajesh Pandey, was among the founding members. During the chase, we in the STF realized that Shriprakash was ahead of his times - he ensured that no one had his photograph, he used

AK-47 and he demanded crores for ransom, unheard of during those days.

Moreover, he used cellular phones. These devices had arrived in the state around 1995, and Shukla was already using them. Electronic surveillance was Greek to us and the idea to tap cellular phones didn't even cross most of our minds. But then, I put together a contraption to listen to cellular conversations and even record them. Electronic surveillance, which is now common in criminal investigations, was developed during the chase of Shriprakash Shukla.

As soon as the relative hinted at the involvement of Shriprakash Shukla and a Bihar gang, senior officers supervising the investigation thought the initial line of the probe may have been wrong. These were new leads and needed to be developed, but the relative was one among the crowd of relatives and the officer did not take down his name or address before the relative disappeared into thin air. The cop on duty may not have realized the importance of the information shared with him, but his seniors wanted to pursue it. More than Shriprakash Shukla, they were keen on exploring the role of the Bihar gang.

In Gorakhpur, police teams began gathering information from the local police. Shriprakash Shukla had several murder cases against his name in Cantonment Police Station. The Lucknow Police learnt from Gorakhpur Police that this young man had emerged and become a terror in a matter of a few years and was already challenging both Shahi and Tiwari to take railway contracts for another mafia – Surajbhan Singh of Bihar. The jigsaw puzzle seemed to be falling into place. Shukla was a foot soldier for Surajbhan. He wanted Shahi and Tiwari to make room for his master in railway tenders.

The headquarters of North-Eastern Railway in Gorakhpur had its catchment area in Bihar. Tenders for railway contracts used to be violent affairs. Musclemen would throng the headquarters when bids were invited. The online tender process that we see today didn't exist in those times. Everything was manual. The forms would be collected, filled and submitted with bids. The contractors hired goons to browbeat their competitors and stop them from participating in the process. The fight for dominance would begin from the time forms were issued to the time of award of contracts. First, people were told not to take forms. If they still took them, they would be told not to submit their bids. This meant not just telling but threatening, and most of the time opening fire to scare. If the scare tactic did not work, there would be murders.

Each contract process had stories of violence. Sometimes, even the officers, who would award the tender, came under attack. The bloodbath did not spare anyone and didn't have any limits. The contractors would go to any lengths to pocket a contract. The process spawned many criminal gangs; Shahi's and Tiwari's were the biggest in those times. It goes without saying that all contracts went to either of them.

Surajbhan, who was a politician from Bihar, had been eyeing a share in this pie for a long time, but the two Gorakhpur men didn't allow him a leeway.

Surajbhan tried a couple of times to break into this league, but failed. One of the reasons was that he didn't have any foot soldiers in Gorakhpur. The other reason was that the two Gorakhpur gangs were too big for him to take on. He was always on the lookout for someone who could challenge the hegemony of Shahi and Tiwari. Shriprakash fit the bill.

Tales of his bravado wafted to Bihar. He was a daring man and had the guts to take on anyone. The crimes and the murder he had committed in Gorakhpur were all sensational. He had killed in broad daylight.

In 1996, Surajbhan got in touch with Shriprakash and gave him an offer – if Shriprakash would get him railway tenders, the Bihar man would sublet work to this young man. It was a lucrative offer because railway contracts meant big money. Also, it meant that Shriprakash would get the patronage of a big, powerful gang. He came on board. It was decided that the first thing they needed to do was to eliminate either of the competition – Shahi or Tiwari – or dominate them. Surajbhan was keen on elimination. They decided to get Shahi out of the picture.

On 22 October 1996, Surajbhan came down with his AK-47 for the mission. Shriprakash, along with Surajbhan and two other henchmen, Anand Pandey and Sudhir Tripathi, drove to their mission in a Maruti Gypsy. When they closed in on the target, Surajbhan handed the automatic assault rifle to Shriprakash.

Shriprakash had a fancy for AK-47. In his mind, he had a picture that with the gun in possession, dominance in crime would be child's play. Ever since he learnt that Surajbhan had the assault rifle, he had been pleading with him to give it to him.

In the Chandralok Lodge attack, Shriprakash tried the gun for the first time.

Although the mission failed, while returning, Surajbhan complimented the Gorakhpur man – "*Tera haath to bada achcha hai* (You have a good hold on the gun)." Surajbhan was impressed.

Shriprakash smiled in gratitude. Secretly, he was dreaming of the day when his master would hand him one such gun for keeps.

Chapter 2
A Riot of Bloodshed

11 January 1997

It was seven in the evening. A hubbub of the calls of hawkers engulfed the market at La Touche Road in Lucknow. This place came to life at early hours, around four in the morning, and remained so till eleven at night. One could witness people squirming on the road at all hours, either to make way for another person or vehicle, or to get through the sea of heads. The ruckus created by the black and yellow three-wheelers, hand carts, rickshaws, two-wheelers and goods carriers was hard to avoid in this crowded part of the city. Vehicles jostled for space on the narrow road. The road connects Charbagh, the hub of railway and roadways transport, to Qaiserbagh and branches off towards Naka Hindola, Paan Dariba, Hewette Road and Aminabad. Lucknow's iconic *chaat wallah*, Tiwari Chaat Bhandar, is also on this road, at a distance of barely 200 metres from the crossroad at Bansmandi. It comes alive in the evenings when people come out for a stroll or to eat out. Dayal Complex, a commercial building built on the land where the old RTO office was situated, is across the road near the roadside eatery. If you are coming from Charbagh Railway Station, it is on the left side after crossing the crossroad at Bansmandi.

All of a sudden, sound of gunshots was heard from near the complex. There was chaos. Within a few minutes, people started running for cover everywhere. Shutters of shops were pulled down and the owners of these establishments remained inside. Some also hurried home. Engines stopped on the roads and the drivers and passengers inside the cars ducked to avoid being accidentally fired upon. No one had any idea what was happening. Within minutes, the road was cleared, and a veil of anticipation descended upon the market. Some said there had been firing inside the complex, and others claimed the bullets had been fired outside it. Some passers-by said they saw three men driving off on a motorbike. They had pistols in hand.

It was a sensational shootout! Who would dare to open fire on this busy street at this time of the day!?

A man lay in a pool of blood near a white Maruti Suzuki 800 outside Dayal Complex. Lottery tickets and casings of bullets were strewn around the body. It was a sight that would remain with the bystanders to haunt them for a very long time. Within minutes, the crowd has dispersed, barring a very few that mostly included shopkeepers, rickshaw-pullers, taxi drivers, fruit and vegetable sellers, etc. They had surrounded the body. Someone from the crowd called the police.

The Naka Police Station was less than a kilometre away. Inspector Ramlal Rai arrived at the crime scene with his team in a matter of minutes after receiving the call. He grunted thinking about the amount of work that this case would require. He knew in his bones that it was not going to be a one-off investigation. This kind of open fire couldn't be the handiwork of some random miscreant. When police arrived, the crowd dispersed and gradually disappeared lest the police should involve them in the investigation, making them eyewitnesses and recording their statements. Mostly, people avoid getting involved in a police investigation for the fear of rounds of courts for evidence during trial and retribution by the criminals involved in those crimes.

I was on my way to Qaisarbagh from Wazirganj. The wireless set hooked to the front bar of the police Gypsy, which had been hissing like a conventional radio not tuned to any particular station, crackled. It was the SSP control room. The booming voice from the other end was alerting all police stations in the city for three men on a motorbike, possibly with weapons in hand.

In about fifteen minutes, news of a shootout on La Touche Road had spread amongst all the police stations in the state. I was the Hazratganj circle officer and the area didn't fall under my jurisdiction, but I instinctively told the driver to take me to the crime spot.

When I reached Dayal Complex, there was a crowd of police officers. Pushing through the throng of curious onlookers, journalists and photographers, I reached the place where the body was lying in a pool of blood. Rai, a stout man, had started formalities; some constables were busy collecting empties of the bullets and senior officers were trying to identify the slain man.

The constables collected thirty-five casings of 9mm and .45mm pistols. The police officers, including myself, were baffled at the use of so many rounds to kill one man, and that too from such close range. Various accounts of the murder were floating in the air. Everyone seemed to have their version of what they had witnessed. Some said that three men were waiting outside the complex. They started firing as soon as the man stepped out.

Some said that the three men engaged in an altercation, after which they had shot the man. But policemen from the local police station, who had received a call about the murder, said someone told them on the telephone that he saw three men dragging a man out of the complex and hurling abuses at him. The man was bleeding and had possibly been shot, but the three shot him again near the man's car before walking to their motorbikes. They also fired some shots in the air to scare the onlookers and to get an easy escape route.

By the time the forensic team arrived and Inspector Rai had told a constable to call an ambulance, the man was identified as twenty-four-year-old Vivek Srivastav, a lottery tycoon, whose office was on the second floor of the complex. The car bearing registration number UP 78 ML 9416, near which the man was lying, was registered in his name. That had helped the police to identify the man. The circle officer and Inspector Rai went to the office of Gangotri Lottery Agency owned by Srivastav. It was deserted. There were bullet marks on the partition in the small ten by ten office. The drawers near the chair where Srivastav sat were stuffed with cash.

Clearly, Srivastav didn't lose his life to robbers. It definitely wasn't murder for loot. If it wasn't for loot, what could it be? The police started from the standard starting point of police investigation of murders – woman, property or rivalry.

Lottery was a booming business in Uttar Pradesh in the late 1990s. Many state governments operated lottery businesses.

Uttar Pradesh also had a directorate of lotteries. Small stalls with canopies all across the city sold paper tickets to people overcome by greed. But one had to be lucky to win anything – and very lucky to win the maximum prize on the ticket. Each ticket had a ten-digit number. The directorates would announce the numbers in the evening. People whose tickets matched all the numbers would walk away with big money; others had to be content with consolations prizes, if they had the same five digits or the same last digit. Most people would be left cursing their luck. The greed for a sudden windfall led to sudden disappointments, but these people would return to the lottery stalls the next day in the hope that the loss of the previous day would be compensated that day. Those who won would also be back to try their luck for bigger amounts. Some became millionaires overnight and some turned paupers.

The business spawned many stars; Vivek Srivastav aka Pinku, as he was locally known, was one of them – and one of the biggest. He started his lottery business with a small stall. In a few years, he rose to become a tycoon, making twenty to thirty lakhs a day. The young man from Malviya Nagar under Bazarkhala Police Station area made big money in a short time. His business partner was a young Punjabi woman named Preeti Kapoor. Some eyewitnesses said she stood near the car when Vivek Srivastav was shot. But she had disappeared before the police arrived. People speculated that she was blinded by the money in the business and wanted to take full control of the lottery agency. She might have hired killers to eliminate her partner.

Vivek Srivastav had everything that a man could possibly aspire for – big money, a beautiful life partner and a more beautiful business partner. He had an affair with Poonam who lived a few houses away. Poonam's brother was a local gangster. Vivek could not have dared to marry a gangster's sister until the brother was out of the picture. Everyone in the neighbourhood was well aware of the exploits of the brother and shuddered at the mention of his name - Akhilesh Rai.

Akhilesh Rai had made a name for himself in the crime circles of Bazarkhala and Naka police stations. He had the reputation of opening fire at the slightest provocation. His cohorts were his friends Vinod Singh and Anil Roberts. They would fire at anyone who tried to belittle or overturn their dominance or violated their writ. But they would not get into petty crimes like theft or burglary. They were big fishes and only had cases of attempt to murder or murders in their names. Police stations had opened history sheets - a police document for habitual offenders to monitor their activities - for Akhilesh.

He was ambitious and wanted to graduate out of the local crime circles. His friend Vinod Singh had already moved over to the nearby township of Rajajipuram. Anil Roberts remained a hanger-on. In due time, Akhilesh Rai got in touch with Surajpal Yadav of the Surajpal gang, a group of dreaded criminals from Gosainganj, a suburban town on Lucknow-Sultanpur Road, to fulfil his ambition. Like all gangsters, Surajpal Yadav had rivalries with other gangs in the city; the gang of Phoolchand Yadav was one of them. Phoolchand of Gudamba was a thorn in Surajpal's flesh.

When Akhilesh approached the Surajpal gang, Surajpal wanted to test Akhilesh before inducting him into the gang. He was asked to eliminate Phoolchand. Akhilesh Rai went to kill Phoolchand on a motorcycle as a pillion rider. He met Phoolchand's brother Shankar and asked, "Where is Phoolchand?"

"Why should I tell you about him? Who are you?" Shankar snapped at Akhilesh Rai.

"Just answer my question or you will be dead in no time," Akhilesh retorted.

"Forget about it. Do you know who I am?"

"Worthless brother of a *namurad* (unsuccessful person)."

"Get the fuck out of this place, you swine!" Shankar hissed.

Akhilesh had pistols in both hands. He shot Shankar in a fit of rage. Thinking that Phoolchand had slipped out, he got back on the bike and while open firing in the air, Akhilesh tried to leave the place. But Phoolchand was there, sitting a few metres away from where Shankar was killed. He had a 315 bore rifle and had perfect aim. The bullet hit Akhilesh Rai's neck.

After riding for about 300 metres, he fell from the motorcycle with a thud. The man riding the bike stopped and on finding Akhilesh Rai dead, sped off to Malviya Nagar to tell Akhilesh Rai's family and friends about the killing. Meanwhile, the Surajpal gang took the body to the police station and hundreds of them gheraoed it. They wanted the man who rode the motorcycle before handing over the body to the family. The impasse ended several hours later and Akhilesh Rai was cremated in Malviya Nagar.

Vivek Srivastav married Poonam two years after his murder.

During the course of investigation, the police found out that Vivek and Poonam's marriage had become patchy over the last few months and they had even contemplated calling it quits. The bone of contention was Vivek's business partner who had slipped into their lives too. Vivek and Preeti were rumoured to be having an affair. Poonam had found out and wanted to walk out of the life of the infidel.

It was first speculated that Akhilesh Rai's friends - Vinod Singh or Anil Roberts - might have killed Vivek Srivastav. However, it was discovered that the same weapon that was used by Akhilesh Rai in Gudamba - 9mm pistols - was used to kill Vivek Srivastav. The forensic team took away the bullet casings to match them with those found in Gudamba three years ago.

The second possible cause that was speculated was a rivalry. Vivek Srivastav may have rubbed many people the wrong way on his road to success; he may have made enemies because of the kind of money he was making. On day two of the investigation, the name of Satya Prakash Pandey alias Sattu Pandey came up. Sattu Pandey was into extortion and police got leads about him threatening Vivek before the killing. Police were also looking into the role of Amit Vishwakarna, a lottery agent, who was close to Vivek and could have tipped off the assailants.

The investigation into the lottery businessman's murder wasn't going anywhere. Many people were suspected and questioned but there wasn't any solid evidence against them. Preeti Kapoor was brought in too, and was questioned and absolved; the bullet casings didn't match with those found in Gudamba and the role of Akhilesh Rai's friends was ruled out. The only motive that police zeroed in on was a business rivalry, but there were no leads about who could be the person behind it.

Barely thirteen days after the sensational killing on the La Touche Road, on 24 January, a triple murder occurred in Alambagh's Tehri Pulia area. The Lucknow Police, already smarting and reeling under the failure to solve Vivek Srivastav's murder, came under insurmountable pressure. Four sensational murders in less than a fortnight! Meetings at police headquarters over Lucknow's law and order situation became a regular affair. Instructions were showered upon everyone from supervisors in the headquarters, especially those in the crime branch. The senior officers used their own network of informers cultivated during their postings in the district police to gather more evidence and clues. The two crimes were from two different police circles but both the teams worked as one, presuming that the same set of criminals had carried out both operations.

The meetings would be preceded by meetings by Lucknow SSP Subesh Kumar Singh. Different teams were following different leads, but all were ultimately hitting roadblocks. For about two months, police followed different tracks which all eventually led to the inference that the two killings were the handiwork of some outside gang.

1 August 1997

Rata-tata-tata-ta...

Dilip Hotel on Hussainganj or Rana Pratap Crossing on Station Road reverberated with the sound of AK-47. Gunshots were heard even in the Vidhan Sabha, which was about five hundred metres away, where a session was underway.

Shriprakash came with aides Anand Pandey and Sudhir Tripathi in a Gypsy with backpacks and asked the receptionist for room number 102. It was on the first floor. While going upstairs to the room, they bumped into a waiter, who was rushing downstairs with a huge pile of dirty laundry. As the waiter collided with Shriprakash, the clothes he was carrying landed on the floor. A pistol emerged from Shriprakash's pocket and he barked at the waiter to knock on the door of room 102. The terrified man followed the orders. The door opened. With lightning speed, Shriprakash opened burst fire from his AK-47 into that tiny room, shouting, "*Bhanuwa kahan hai* (Where is Bhanu)?"

Bullets pierced the freshly painted yellow walls. The room, filled with cement dust, became dark. Sudhir and Anand were also firing from their pistols. They couldn't spot anyone because of the plaster flakes, so they fired indiscriminately. Then they upended the bed, chucking away the mattress and sheets. When the dust settled, they saw a man on the floor; others had probably locked themselves in the bathroom.

Other guests on that floor rushed out of their rooms on hearing gunshots. They started running helter-skelter and the corridor became abuzz with chaos.

Shriprakash decided it was time to return. On their way out, they stopped at the reception. The receptionist was hiding under the table, frozen. "If you commit the mistake of informing the police, you will also be killed," Shriprakash snarled at him and stepped out.

About fifteen minutes later, the receptionist plucked some courage, came out to see if the attackers had gone or not, and when he didn't spot them, he called the police from a public telephone. He could barely splutter – "*Bahut goliyan chali hain, jaldi aaiye.* (Please come soon, a lot of bullets have been fired.)"

Terrified to death, he murmured the location on the phone and disconnected quickly.

I had been transferred out of Hazratganj on 10 June 1997 and was then the Circle Officer of Qaisarbagh. We wasted no time and rushed to Dilip Hotel. We were among the first teams to reach there. SSP Rajnikant Mishra followed, and in a short while, even DGP Shriram Arun came there. It was a sensational shootout, and so close to the Assembly!

There were four men in the room; one of them was Bhanu Mishra. They were rushed to medical college. Another one of them, Vivek Shukla, was declared brought dead. Shriprakash, it seemed, came looking for Bhanu because we were told that he was shouting his name. Bhanu had a bullet injury on his hand but he could talk. He was hiding in the bathroom with two other men.

He told us that someone called Ashok Singh would often call him and warn him to not get into railway tenders. He said that after Shahi's murder, all tenders in his name would be taken by him. "Who do you think you are? Even Hari Shankar Tiwari won't dare to get into this," he would say threatening Bhanu with death.

When Ashok Singh called Bhanu for the first time, Bhanu made inquiries in the local crime circle – there was no one big by that name. Thinking that someone was trying to pull a fast one on him, Bhanu ignored the calls.

"But today when the AK-47 was spewing bullets, the man kept saying, '*Shriprakash se dushmani bahut mahengi padegi* (It would cost you dear to be Shriprakash's enemy)," Bhanu told us. This was an important piece of information. There was a common link among the three murders: Shriprakash.

When we were speaking with Bhanu in the hospital, there was a call at the SSP office.

"Jai Hind, SSP office," a constable answered.

"Has there been a shootout in Lucknow?" An exasperated caller asked.

Without introducing himself, the man spoke further – "Someone called me to announce that my brother, Bhanu Mishra, was dead and that I should rush to Lucknow with white cloth for the bier. We are starting from Gorakhpur, but we wanted to cross-check if a shootout had indeed taken place in Lucknow."

"I am not aware of any shootout," the constable replied nonchalantly. He wasn't aware of the Dilip Hotel shootout yet. The line went dead.

Soon, wireless sets began buzzing. When the constable finally learnt about the shootout and heard frenetic messages on the set, he thought it necessary to inform the SSP about the call from Gorakhpur.

He went into the SSP's chamber and knocked urgently.

"Come in! There is no need to break the door," the SSP roared.

"Sir, I have a piece of information. Earlier, I had got a call related to the shootout. The caller said that he was Bhanu Mishra's brother from Gorakhpur." The constable narrated the entire phone conversation to the SSP.

The SSP, who had a file open before him, looked up and acknowledged with a nod. He seemed uninterested in the information.

The constable got the hint and came out.

Bhanu's family reached Lucknow in the evening and went straight to the medical college. The SSP had told us about the call from Gorakhpur. We took his brother aside and asked him about the call that he said he received from Lucknow.

The call on his landline had come around 11 a.m. "The caller identified himself as Shriprakash and declared that he had killed Bhanu. He said, '*Kafan lekar aao, lash le jao* (Come with the white cloth and take his body).' We got worried. I called SSP Gorakhpur. He wasn't aware of any shootout. He suggested that I call the office of SSP Lucknow. He was the one who gave me the number. We were also calling Bhanu simultaneously but in vain. Our nephew, who was with Bhanu, and their driver - everyone was inaccessible," he told us.

Three big murders got Lucknow Police in knots. During the investigation of the Shahi murder case, police found links to suggest that Shriprakash was behind killing Vivek Srivastav too. Vivek's cousin's husband, Subhash Tripathi, was a lottery businessman. He had some stalls in Qaiserbagh, but wanted to expand. He had been requesting Vivek Srivastav for dealership of the area. He was also seeking twenty per cent share in the business on the Cantonment Road. The lottery tycoon obviously didn't want to share his fortunes. Tripathi discussed this with Shriprakash during one of his Lucknow visits. Shriprakash was looking for an opportunity to graduate from Gorakhpur's crime world to that of the state capital.

Vivek Srivastav proved to be his first assignment in Lucknow. He killed the lottery tycoon with two accomplices, Anand Pandey and Siriya Pahelwan.

But the Dilip Hotel shootout was the most sensational. It was for the first time in Lucknow's history that an AK-47 had been used in a crime. The use of this sophisticated weapon so close to the Assembly and at a time when the Hussainganj crossing was chock-a-block with traffic, was alarming. Dilip Hotel was on the Vidhan Sabha Road, one of Lucknow's arterial roads, connecting Alambagh to trans-Gomti areas. To open fire on such a road and at the peak hours of the day requires immense guts.

Police were also scandalised by the number of rounds fired in each of these killings. Using fifty to sixty rounds to kill one man! That was something! This had been the same pattern of killings of lottery tycoon Vivek Srivastav, mafia don Virendra Pratap Shahi and Vivek Shukla. The purpose, the police concluded, was to create terror. For Shriprakash, the location didn't matter. He could strike at any place, without an iota of fear. The man clearly wanted to arrive in the Lucknow scene with a bang. The Dilip Hotel shootout, in which his name emerged loud and clear, proved that he had been successful.

During the Dilip Hotel shootout investigation, more police teams were dispatched to Gorakhpur. The teams investigating the Shahi murder case were already there. When police linked Shriprakash to the lottery murder case, the team working on the Vivek Srivastav case was also roped in. The three sensational cases had only one suspect – Shriprakash Shukla.

Bhanu's brother had been called soon after the shootout. We thought the assailants must have used a nearby PCO. Hoping that the PCO operator could describe the person to us, we hopped from one PCO to the other within a five-km radius of Dilip Hotel. The Gorakhpur number had not been called from any of them.

We also got in touch with the telecom officials in Qaisarbagh. They confirmed that a landline phone had not been used to make the call to Bhanu's brother. They said a cellular phone could have been used.

Cellular phone? We had only heard about it, but never used it. How did Shriprakash become an early subscriber of the service?

Cellular services were launched in the east UP circle when I was posted as Hazratganj CO, but until then mobile phone devices were a rarity. The two companies that got the cellular license – Usha Phone and Essar – were in their infancy, setting up towers, rolling out plans and adding subscribers. The service was very expensive – an outgoing call would cost seventeen rupees a minute and the incoming call was charged at ten rupees for the same duration.

Usha Phone was launched in Lucknow on 31 March 1997, and the Essar showroom opened in May.

The elder son of Ram Narayan Sahu, a big Lucknow businessman and a politician, opened the Essar showroom across the road in front of Hazratganj Kotwali. Sahu invited the then SSP Subesh Kumar Singh and me to the inauguration. After the ceremony, he gifted both of us a mobile set each. The sets had active SIM cards. Sahu scribbled the ten-digit cell numbers on small chits and gave them to us.

"For now, you can only call cellular numbers in the Hazratganj area," he said, "but you can call on any landline number anywhere." The sets lay in our cars for several days.

One day, when I was sitting with the SSP in his office, he said, "Let's check and test the cellular phones."

"Sure. Let me tell someone to fetch them for us."

When the phones were brought, he passed on the cellular phone to me.

"Call my office. I have been getting complaints that the personnel on telephone duty in the office doesn't connect callers to me."

"Really? It can bear great repercussion if he chooses not to connect an important call."

"Let's verify the complaint," the SSP said as I began dialling on the swanky handset. The call didn't get through. The SSP got angry.

"Didn't he say we can call all landlines from this?" he asked me. I nodded in agreement.

"Call Sahu to come and collect these. Only you and I have these sets. If we cannot call landline numbers, these are of no use – how much will you and I talk?"

I called Sahu from the landline and informed him that the cellular phones weren't working. He asked me if I had prefixed the landline number with Lucknow's STD code. I hadn't.

The next call was made to the same landline with prefixed STD code and it went through. The SSP took the phone from me and asked if the SSP was in office. The man at telephone duty said no and asked about the caller.

Smiling at me, the SSP said, "How does that matter? I may be anyone. I need to speak to the SSP." And then he said, "*Achcha tum undar aao* (Come inside)."

The constable realized it was the SSP himself. He came in sheepishly, looking puzzled.

"*Tum sab ko bol dete ho main office me nahi hoon* (You tell everyone that I am not in office)? I don't want this to happen again. If I hear this again, you would have had it," the SSP said.

The constable hadn't seen a cellular phone before. He was looking at the set in the SSP's hands.

"I have called the number from this cellular phone. Change is around. Better watch it!" SSP warned him.

Chapter 3
The Elusive Photograph

They say that a small piece of information may unveil a lot. The Mishras in Gorakhpur after the shootout at Dilip Hotel got a call from a cellular phone. This was a vital piece of information.

SSP Rajnikant Mishra looked straight into my eyes and said, "We need to find out the cellular number."

Luckily, the head of Usha Phone in Lucknow, RK Singh, had been my classmate at Allahabad University. We had not been in touch, but I was sure he would help us. Even otherwise, he would anyway have to cooperate with a police investigation.

When I contacted him and we were through with the catching up, I told him that we were looking for a cellular number used in a crime.

"I am not a technical man," he said. "Give me two-three days. I'm sure my technical team can find this out."

A few days later, RK Singh called. "The number has been found," he said. "We have all the details. Please come so that I can give them to you."

"But please don't come in police uniform," he requested. "When people see police entering an office, they get vile ideas and make stories. It would be better that you come in civvies."

Incidentally, both the SSP and I were in a civil dress that day.

"Let's go and get it," SSP Mishra said urgently. The Usha Phone office at Shriram Tower on Shahnajaf Road was a few metres from the SSP office. We walked to the office.

Singh gave us about twenty-five pages of computer printouts. The pages had details of numbers called from the cellular phone – along with each call's duration – since the connection was taken. The connection was in the name of Ram Naresh Shukla, a politician from Pratapgarh. The electricity bill of the politician's house in Vinay Khand had been submitted to the company as proof of address.

We began working on the voluminous data and found that Shriprakash also used pagers to convey messages to his men in Lucknow. Pager, a small messaging device, was launched around six months before the cellular phones arrived. It was a status symbol at that time. People would hook it to their belts. Newspapers gave it to their reporters to let the editors communicate with them through the day.

Shriprakash would drop messages on pager for his men to call him from PCOs. Until then, police only worked on local or manual intelligence. It was before the electronic surveillance era. Cellular services would work only in some pockets as installation of towers was still underway in Lucknow and other cities.

We went to the pager office at Chintel House to learn about the technology. The corporation was hesitant to disclose any information. They claimed that it constituted an invasion of the clients' privacy. We explained that we were agencies in need of information for an investigation. We stated that they were obligated to deliver it to us. They gave in, but the pager information was useless. The next day, I was waiting for the SSP at his office. About half an hour later, he stormed into the room and announced that we should raid Ram Naresh Shukla's house in Vinay Khand. We started preparing immediately and discussed our plan. The SSP said he would be a part of the raid. SP City Satyendra Vir Singh and I tried to dissuade him, but he didn't listen to us.

The head of the technical team at Usha Phone had told us that the location of Shriprakash's cellular phone was on the tower near the house until three days ago. The phone had been switched off, but we presumed that Shriprakash may still be around and planned the raid.

Everyone put on their bulletproof jackets and raided the house around midnight. There was one woman and two girls in the house. The house was searched. We got hold of an important lead – Shriprakash did stay in that house.

It was the first time that we could surely say that Shriprakash was behind these sensational crimes. But he was like a mirage. All we had was a name. No one knew how he looked. No one had a photograph of him.

This caused us embarrassment in meetings at the DG office. Senior officers mocked us – "You don't even know how he looks; how will you solve the cases." The meetings started to feel suffocating. We didn't have anything in the name of progress in the investigation, apart from a name.

"This investigation is heading nowhere. We are stuck," one of the senior officers declared.

"It will not progress even an inch until," he turned and pointed towards me and SSP Mishra, and said, "you know how he looks. Find his photo first." He continued, "We need his photo for the 'wanted' posters and to circulate among the police stations."

The search began in Gorakhpur. We used our network to enquire from the Tiwari and the Shahi gangs. They didn't have a photograph. Small-time criminals who had had links with Shriprakash - Kishori Lal, Nilendra Pandey, Ghanshyam Pathak aka Dhannu - were of no use too.

Video shoots at weddings had been a new craze in those days. We began contacting photographers, who doubled up as videographers, in the hope that we may get him in a wedding shoot. Some photographers were picked, but they were reluctant to share anything. They said that Shriprakash was a deadly man and if he found out that any of them had shared his photo with the police, he may kill them.

The fear was not unfounded. A photographer was shot. Shriprakash had pumped bullets into his body.

"You think you can distribute my photo to the police?" he barked in rage as he pulled the trigger of his pistol.

Shriprakash was aware that without a photograph, the police wouldn't be able to do much against him. He didn't like to be clicked. And if someone did click his picture, he would threaten him with murder if it went to the police.

The search in Gorakhpur had been unsuccessful. The police teams returned to Lucknow. The quest for the photograph led us to Subhash Tiwari, a relative of Shriprakash, whose name had cropped up in the Vivek Srivastav case. We went to his house on Prayag Narain Road in Hazratganj. We raided the house and didn't allow Subhash Tripathi to escape.

"What's your relationship with Shriprakash?" We shot the first question.

He was reluctant to talk, but the presence of a heavy police force disarmed him. He said Shriprakash was his wife's cousin.

"When did he visit you last?"

"A few months ago," he said.

"Give us his photo."

He said he didn't have any photos.

We threatened to book him for providing shelter to a criminal. "All of you will be behind bars," we threatened, thinking that the fear of arrest may work the trick. But it didn't.

While we were questioning him, his daughter walked into the room. "Beta, do you know Shriprakash Shukla?" a woman constable asked.

"Yes," she said. "He is my mama."

We sent the parents to another room and started chatting with her.

After general queries about her school, we asked her about her hobbies. She said she was fond of photography.

"Do you have a camera?"

"Yes, my mama gifted me one on my birthday," she said in excitement and ran inside to bring the camera.

"Here," she said showing it to us.

"Did you click anything?"

"Yes. I clicked photos on my birthday," she said and went in again to bring some photos tucked into a notebook.

She had had her birthday fifteen days ago. Subhash Tripathi had lied to us. Shriprakash was here just two weeks ago.

We looked at the photographs. There were her parents and some friends. In one photograph, a handsome man also stood in the frame.

"This?" we looked at the girl inquisitively.

"That's my mama."

Shriprakash!

We got hold of a photograph. Finally!

Her parents were probably eavesdropping on the conversation. They rushed out and fell at our feet.

"If you use this photo anywhere, he will know the source and kill all of us," the man said beseeching us.

"Why will he kill you? You are his brother-in-law."

"Relations don't mean anything for him," they said. "Haven't you seen how mercilessly he kills people? We are a small family. He will destroy us. Please don't use this photograph," they began hollering.

The girl saw his parents begging and crying. She must have realized that she had done something wrong. She also began crying.

But we couldn't let go of this important discovery. We took the photograph anyway.

On our way back, Satyendra Vir Singh and I discussed that the family may actually be in danger if this photo was used. Then there would be another murder and more pressure on the police. The two of us were trying to figure out a way to avoid this.

"Can we do something to change the background?" I asked Satyendra Vir Singh.

"You have been CO Hazratganj and now you are in Qaisarbagh. All the big shops are in these two police areas. You figure out how this can be done."

"I surely will," I replied confidently, although I had no idea how to go about it.

He dropped me outside the Hanuman Mandir near Hazratganj Kotwali. I thought of checking out the stalls on the pavement from Universal Booksellers to Coffee House. The stalls sold goggles, postcards, magazines and other sundry items. Walking past one of them, my eyes fell on one postcard of Sunil Shetty which looked eerily familiar to the photo that I had. I bought the postcard and walked to Amar Fax near the office of CO Hazratganj. That was the only colour photocopy facility in Lucknow at that time. Bunty, its owner, knew me since my days as CO.

"I want to paste the head of this man in the photograph on Suniel Shetty's torso and take out photocopies." Bunty looked at the man in the photograph and got cold feet.

"*Bhaiyya, mar dega* (Brother, he will kill me)."

"*Kuch nahi hone wala hai. Tumhe police protect karegi* (Nothing will happen to you. The police will protect you)."

He decided to do it himself, as he did not trust any of his staff with the sensitive and confidential work. We went to his chamber. Shriprakash's head from the original photo was cut and pasted on Sunil Shetty's torso. It was almost a perfect fit.

The photo was put in the photocopy machines and 100 to 200 copies were printed on glossy sheets. I went to the SSP with these sheets. The officer was informed about the manipulation and the reason for it.

There was a big press conference that evening. The SSP released the photo to the media. The next day, it was on the front page of all newspapers. And there was relief in the police department that finally we had a face to the dreaded name.

To date, this is the only photo of the gangster available anywhere.

Chapter 4
The Janpath Murder

After three shootouts in Lucknow, the cops were under tremendous pressure. The only success we had was an image of Shriprakash, whom we suspected was responsible for the crimes. We were confirming all information that came our way, no matter how big or small. Some people came up with information on their own, including some astute inspectors and sub-inspectors. It was decided that we would compile every detail and verify it to get the bigger picture. We got together every morning to exchange notes and divided work among us to verify the information. The teams were told that if they spotted anyone matching Shriprakash's profile, they were not to act alone. "Inform others. We will take any action only when we are a big force," they were told. Everyone was given the photograph, and the instruction of not acting alone was repeated several times.

The constables from Gorakhpur and Deoria who knew that Shriprakash got agitated on learning that someone had his photograph and refused to carry it with them. For four months, all his rivals - whether it was Hari Shankar Tiwari or Virendra Pratap Shahi's men or Kishori Lal's gang - had failed to find his photograph. "Whoever is found with my photo will be killed," Shriprakash had announced. Hence, the constables said they would identify the man even without the photo, but would not risk their lives by carrying a photograph around. We got to know about the constables' hesitation much later.

After the Dilip Hotel shootout, we had contacted telecom officials to find out which number had been used to call Bhanu Mishra's family in Gorakhpur. We got hold of Shriprakash's call detail record (CDR). Some PCO numbers figured in it. Before the floodgates of mobile phones were opened and unleashed to the world, there used to be a row of PCOs on the pavement across the road outside Indira Bhawan, Jawahar Bhawan and Shakti Bhawan - the three big government offices of Lucknow. People used to call employees and officials working in these buildings from the small cubicles. The other cluster of PCOs was near the Qaisarbagh crossing. There were PCOs in the market in front of Kotwali too.

We asked the telecom officials to suggest ways to find out the call details of the four numbers that we had zeroed in on from the analysis of the CDR. We asked them if there was a way we could listen to those calls. They agreed to give us parallel lines from telephone poles.

"Find a safe place from where you can discreetly listen to the conversations on these numbers," they said.

That was how it was done by the state agencies - string out parallel lines from telephone poles, rent lodgings or pitch a tent in the vicinity and listen to calls. "The target might get to know due to the disturbance in the phone," they warned us.

We couldn't hire a commercial space for this operation because it may let out our secret. People would then start wondering which numbers we were tapping and why. The newspapers would present the town with a juicy, scandalous scoop. People, whose conversations we wanted to tap, would be alerted and there could be an embarrassment for the police.

The telecom officials said, "When we repair telephone lines, we generally pitch tents near the poles. Sometimes, the tents remain there for as long as ten days."

An idea struck us.

"Can you get us two tents, one near the SSP office to listen to Hazratganj numbers, and the other in front of SP City's residence in Qaisarbagh?" we asked them. The answer was obviously yes.

Three constables on an eight-hour duty each were deputed in the tents. The mouthpieces of the telephone receivers were taped by several layers of cellophane to filter outside noise. The constables were told to pick the receiver before it was picked at the other end. We realized that if the person on the other end was smart enough, then the person could easily pick the noise of the receiver going off the cradle. And this may give them a heads-up about their phones being on surveillance.

We were told that the constables would get a ring whenever the number would be used to dial or receive calls. In the CDR, there were numbers of two PCOs each in Qaiserbagh and Hazratganj. We were interested in listening to all conversations from these numbers. The good news was that these were PCO numbers and people in PCOs were used to noise during calls, so there were fewer chances that the targets would find out about phone surveillance.

A little background, I feel, is necessary at this point to tell you how primitive was phone tapping back in those days. I had got a telecom engineer in Allahabad to devise a typewriter-sized interception box, which was lugged around and connected to switching stations. Until then, calls could only be listened to, not recorded. I also devised a recording kit. A kit from the electronic market behind Naka Police Station was fixed on the receiver near the mouthpiece where the twisted cable went in. One cable went into the landline phone and the other into a tape recorder. The kit cost ₹125. The tape would record all the conversations when switched on.

After his photo was published in the newspapers, the constables listened to a call from one of the four numbers. Shriprakash asked for a certain man who was already waiting at the PCO.

"Bhaiyya, all newspapers here have your photo on the front page," the man from Lucknow PCO said.

"That's impossible. Did you see it yourself? What am I wearing?"

"You are wearing a denim shirt."

"I don't wear denim shirts. People in Bombay and Delhi wear it. I don't wear such clothes because I will be easily identified if I wore them."

"Bhaiyya, it is undoubtedly your photo. And a very clear one, at that," the man from Lucknow persisted.

There was silence on the other side for a moment.

Then he said, "Ok! Collect all newspapers with my photo and go to the Gomti Nagar police station crossing the day after. I will have them collected."

"*Thik hai, bhaiyya* (All right, brother)," the Lucknow PCO man said and disconnected the call.

The constables called us. They told us about the phone conversation. We got cracking and found out that the call had come from a Nepal landline number. The Gorakhpur team was sent to Nepal to find out more. It turned out to be a PCO in Kathmandu.

Meanwhile, our teams looked for people associated with him, people who wandered with him, went to movies. They told us two things – first, he lusts after girls and second, after every two to three days, he goes to a salon for a shave. He went to high-end salons where lowly cops were unlikely to get access. Only four police officers had seen him and could identify him. They were sub-inspectors Ram Rekha Yadav, Parmanand Dubey, Parshuram Singh and Jayant Yadav. They had seen the ganglord when he surrendered in 1993 and was in jail for five months. This was the only time in his grisly career of five years that he was behind bars.

In a couple of days, I got a call from one of my informers.

"Hello, sir. *Pata lag chukka hai who kahan jata hai* (I know where he goes)."

"Come to my house and let me know. It is not safe to talk about such matters over the telephone. Come tomorrow at 6 a.m."

He told me that Shriprakash went to the salon at Taj Hotel. We went there with his photograph. The man there identified him and said he came very often and gave heavy tips. The shave cost around ₹150, but he would always pay the man ₹200. Maybe he wanted to ensure that he didn't say anything when anyone came inquiring about him, we thought.

We also learnt that he spent his evenings at the Janpath market, especially at Chhedilal Juice Corner, which was at the entry to the market from the Hazratganj side. He would sit outside the juice shop for hours, staring at women lustfully. Sometimes, he would visit the shops, especially the chikan stores, where women came for shopping.

His routine also included going to KD Singh Babu Stadium every morning, at around five in the morning, in a tracksuit, carrying a badminton bag. When we enquired about him from a few people, they said that he jogged for a while and then sat on the stairs near the court where women played. He stared at them and sometimes even passed some lewd comments.

Shriprakash was a careful man, but his lustful folly gave him away. We learnt that he often visited primary schools to make a pass at mothers who came to drop their young children. Post returning from the stadium, he would go to any of these schools. He would go to Mahanagar Boys, Karamat or St Francis and Loreto in Hazratganj.

With this little piece of information, the police department was again abuzz with speculations.

Is it his sole motive to visit schools? Is he planning to kidnap the child of a rich businessman?

Our informers later told us that he was against kidnapping young ones. "They are difficult to manage and if they die, there's no bigger sin," our informers learnt this from someone in Shriprakash's gang.

We now had some clue about where and how we could swoop down on him. He was also spotted quite a few times at Bombay Hair Cutting Salon in Janpath. Whenever he would not go to Taj – we were informed – he would come here.

SP City Satyendra Vir Singh had a light-green Maruti 800. Every evening, he, his gunner Rankendra and I would get into the car in plain clothes and go to Janpath to look for people with big bags. The information was that Shriprakash never stepped out without his AK-47 which he carried in a cricket kit bag. We were hoping to catch him.

Around 6.30 p.m., on 9 September 1997, Satyendra said he had some information and asked us to get ready for the evening jaunt. It had been four or five days since we were going there, but in vain.

The offices of SP City and CO Qaisarbagh used to be adjacent to each other in the same building. We often sat together poring over numbers on the CDR. We found landline numbers of Bihar, Bombay, Darjeeling and Nepal. We would call the telecom officials in those districts to get a call summary. The analysis used to be done manually back then - numbers were either marked green or red using pens. There were no Excel sheets to filter numbers for us.

A constable called Ravindra worked on the numbers. He would analyze how many calls were made to which number, what were the durations of those calls, etc., and used to send us the details in the evening.

RK Singh was SP City's reader - very humble and extremely resourceful. He was in charge of allotment and management of VIP duties, duties during festivals and other events, and was also responsible for granting leave. All inspectors, sub-inspectors and constables knew him. RK Singh diligently collated sundry information that need to be sent to the DG office - some daily and some every fortnight - and ensured that every report was sent on time. He also worked on the numbers to track Shriprakash.

"We are going to Janpath. You stay here," Satyendra Singh told RK Singh that evening. But RK Singh wanted to accompany the evening party. He said he was anyway planning to go to Murari Bapu Katha, a recital of the Ramayana, at Eldeco Green Park, an upscale township in Gomti Nagar, after winding up work. He requested the SP City to arrange two passes for him. The katha was to begin at 9 p.m. and RK Singh hoped to be home before that.

The four of us – Satyendra Vir Singh, Rankendra, RK Singh and I – reached Janpath and parked the car near Darul Shafa. The initial plan was that we would split into two teams, each manning the two entries to the market. But it was later decided not to split and be one team. We went to Bombay Hair Cutting Salon. RK Singh went in and looked around. He came out and said there was no one matching Shriprakash's description.

The shops in Janpath market are around a raised platform; there are shops underneath the platform, and on the ground floor of the platform. We did two rounds of the market and were getting out through a small alleyway around 8 p.m. RK Singh stayed back. We thought probably he had seen something suspicious or saw someone with a bag. We had barely entered the gallery when we came face to face with a man with a big bag. He was himself a small man and looked like a misfit with the heavy bag. He looked unusual. Satyendra Vir Singh stopped him and told him to open it. He became fidgety and was reluctant. Of course, he did not know that we were cops in plain clothes.

The man nervously looked around while trying to reach for the zip. Satyendra Vir Singh brought out his pistol and started working his way around the zip. Finally, I opened it. The man yanked himself out of Satyendra Vir Singh's grip and ran. He ran into Topandas's Lucknow Chikan shop. The bag had an AK-47. We left it in Rankendra's custody and ran behind the man. The man fell in the shop. Rankendra followed us in. He also had his pistol in his hand.

There was pandemonium. The man leapt at Rankendra's pistol and gripped it tightly. We were shocked at his brazenness. We had pinned him down and were kicking him, but he wouldn't let go of the pistol. We dragged him out and shot him in the leg. The grip went limp only after this.

Before we would interrogate him, there was news that someone had been shot several times and killed near Darul Shafa. Hearing the gunfire, the local police from Hazratganj Police Station also reached the spot. They dumped the man with AK-47 in the police jeep and whisked him off to the nearest police station. We dashed towards Darul Shafa to check out the other criminal. We thought this may have been RK Singh's target.

The man on the ground lay lifeless. He must have been shot barely minutes ago in his head. When we saw the man, we got the shock of our lives. It was RK Singh!

He lay on his stomach, the chord of his pistol stretching out of his body. We felt dizzy and unsteady. Completely at our wit's end. Absolutely numb.

He was put in the car and taken to a medical college, but RK Singh was already dead.

News of this murder spread like wildfire. Janpath is a busy marketplace in the heart of Hazratganj. Hundreds of people visit it for shopping and evening strolls. RK Singh's death was a rude shock. Since 1 August 1997, he was with us like a shadow, working on numbers, briefing teams, collecting information. He was meticulous with his work. We lost him right in front of our eyes.

Subesh Kumar was the SSP. He reached the spot a few minutes later. All police stations were informed about the shootout and instructed to set up barricades. We were about to leave Janpath when we received information that a black backpack was found unattended on the stairs of B Block in Darul Shafa. The informer said it was full of weapons. We rushed back. The bag had one carbine, two small weapons and a large number of cartridges.

Darul Shafa is the official accommodation for legislators. A new cabinet had been sworn in and many ministers were present in the building that evening. The officer-in-charge of the Darul Shafa police outpost was also there. After the preliminary investigation, we found that the bag was not there until an hour ago. The bag was spotted only half an hour back. That meant there was a difference of twenty minutes between the crime and the discovery of the bag.

We were sure the man must be in the building. He either threw the bag after finding refuge or left it on the staircase before getting into someone's flat. There was some ray of hope. We thought we would bring home success, even though we had lost RK Singh.

The police force from the entire city surrounded Darul Shafa. Every room, every kitchen, every toilet was searched. There were offices of some small political parties. Some ministers were also there because they hadn't been allotted bungalows. The search lasted for an hour and a half, but we got hold of no one.

We went back to the spot to find out what may have happened. Some eyewitnesses said, "We saw the *daroga ji* (colloquial word for sub-inspectors in UP) chasing three men." This happened when we were busy with the man with AK-47. "He had a pistol in hand and was screaming at them."

During the chase, his feet got snared in three rows of wire in the parking lot and he fell. The wires were used to demarcate the parking lot and to ensure people didn't leave without paying the parking fee. They were simple wires, not barbed ones, rising to two feet.

The three men had entered Darul Shafa gate when RK Singh fell. They realized that RK Singh had fallen. They immediately returned. One of them kicked him in the back when he was trying to get up and the other two snatched his pistol. They placed the muzzle of the gun to his temple and shot him point-blank several times. Then they fled with the weapon.

People on the second and third floors of Darul Shafa could have witnessed the shooting. There were security personnel on almost all floors, all with their rifles towards Janpath. They must have surely witnessed the men who shot RK Singh dead. But no one came forward to report. The ordinary people on the street couldn't have taken the criminals on, but they could at least inform the police about it. There must have been at least a thousand people in the market and at least five hundred at the spot where RK Singh was shot, but no one was willing to share anything with us.

The next morning, at the postmortem house, there was a huge turnout of police personnel. The family was inconsolable. There was an army of journalists too. When a man emerged out of the postmortem facility, ten to twenty journalists lunged forward. The man said there were nine bullets in RK Singh's body. He had a Hanuman Chalisa book in his pocket, a wallet with some money and a photograph of Shriprakash Shukla. The journalists got the breaking news and left.

After the autopsy, the body was taken to the police line with full government honour. There, at least a thousand police personnel had turned out to bid their final adieu to RK Singh. SSP Subesh Kumar Singh, DIG Kashmir Singh and all other police officers were present. It was a very emotional scene. Satyendra Vir Singh noticed that the SSP had his head down and was probably in tears. Satyendra Singh signalled me to follow him to where the SSP was standing. When we went closer, we found him sobbing bitterly. He was a strong man and was never known to be overwhelmed by emotions. He didn't speak to us, got into his car and left. We went behind him. When we pulled into the SSP residence, his car was in the portico. We went to him just when he was about to get off his car. His eyes were red with tears. He didn't utter a single word, just signalled to us to leave.

The SSP was broken. He called us the next day and said we needed to take revenge for RK Singh's killing. This was the fourth sensational crime in the city. RK Singh kept nine bullets in the magazine. The criminals had pumped all into his head.

The newspapers had screaming headlines about the murder of a sub-inspector in a busy marketplace.

The headline in a Hindi daily read – *Rajdhani me sarkar ki nak ke neeche sub-inspector ki sansanikhez hatya* (a sub-inspector is killed in the capital although the force was present). Reporters wrote about how Shriprakash could have escaped.

We had the information. We were going and making rounds there for five days, and yet, we couldn't get the man. What was worse, we lost one of our officers. The prestige of UP Police was at stake.

It was an insurmountable loss, but we had to get on with our routine from the next day. The bag from the first man had an AK-47, fifty cartridges and a diary. He turned out to be Surajbhan's most trusted shooter, Tuniyaram, from Mokama. Shriprakash got him to Lucknow a few days ago. Surajbhan didn't give him his AK-47 and said Shriprakash already has one. Tuniyaram came to Lucknow via Gorakhpur and Faizabad and was here for the last three days.

Chapter 5
The Moolraj Arora Kidnapping

Shriprakash did not sit silently after the horrifying murders. Instead, he focused on strengthening his information network to gather information about new targets – people who had money, traders, businessmen, doctors, owners of coaching centres, etc. He was looking for people from whom he could extort money.

One day, Shriprakash, Anand and Sudhir were discussing ways to make money. They said they needed money to buy more weapons. "After killing Shahi and the police sub-inspector, we have arrived in the crime circuit and established ourselves in the underworld. Now we need money to expand," Shriprakash said. Others nodded in agreement. They decided to shift to kidnapping, the shortcut to making big money in one fell swoop.

For this, the gang needed to identify potential targets before kidnapping them. They already had an army of young men, mostly students and in their early twenties, from Gorakhpur and nearby areas. Shriprakash gave them pagers, provided them with two-wheelers with valid documentation and put them on the job of preparing *kundali* (horoscope).

He called it *kundali nikalna.* The modus operandi was simple. The men would be given a number, or address and told to find out everything about that person in three to four days. The number or address (of shop or residence) was given through pager and the information, when gathered, had to be shared back through this device only.

The men would follow the target and learn about their routine - when did he leave his house, in which vehicle, how many people were with him, where did he go, what time he reach his shop or office, who all came to meet him, when did he come out, where did he have lunch, if he went home for having lunch or not, what time he came, what time he returned, who opened the door for him, how much time he spent at home, and so on. It had to be a very detailed kundali. If someone provided short or incomplete information, Shriprakash would get angry. He would say they hadn't found out about *Rahu* and *Ketu*. Later, we discovered that this was a code word for security guards flanking the targets.

The men worked assiduously to gather information about the targets. In exchange, they were given money. If someone gave him good information, he would ask that person to go to a particular place and say that Ashok bhaiyya had sent him. The other person would hand them either 2,000 rupees or 5,000 rupees, depending upon the quality of information or the importance of the target. Shriprakash valued detailed kundalis. He would pay them more money. Most of these men were students in Lucknow University or had come to the capital for coaching. They came from modest families and craved a good lifestyle. Those who had girlfriends needed money to splurge on them. Shriprakash loosened his purse strings for them. Five thousand rupees was a handsome amount in those days. Some even got 7,000 for one kundali.

When they ran out of money, a message would pop on Sudhir's pager - "*Bhaiyya, bahut din se koi kaam nahi bataya hai* (you haven't given us work for many days.)" Shriprakash would give them random names to prepare kundali, sometimes just to humour them.

The targets were called in the evening. Around 9 p.m., Shriprakash would rattle off the person's routine that day - you left home at this time and reached a particular place at this time. "I was there," he would say, "and I could have killed you. You have a lot of money. Give me this amount." The person would be taken aback.

One such incident happened with the owner of a Raymond store. He told him his routine with such minute details that he became speechless. "You went to Prakash Kulfi after closing the shop. You ordered six kulfis. You didn't take it and asked the person at the counter to get it delivered to your car. A man brought the kulfi in a polythene packet. You told him to keep it in the back seat. When you went home, your elderly servant opened the door for you and you gave him the car keys before going upstairs. The servant parked the car in the garage."

This shook the ground from under the shop owner's feet. 'My god! He knows so much about me,' he thought.

People didn't inform the police. Some of them paid the ransom while some negotiated for a smaller amount. If he asked for a sum of twenty lakhs, they would settle for five lakhs to wriggle out of his clutches. He even knew about people sitting in the offices of police officers. He would say to some of them, "I know you spend too much time in SP City's office."

The people who received the call would be flummoxed with the kind of detail he had about them. He seemed to know everything about them. "If you report this to the police or if this comes out in the newspapers, you will be dead. I will shoot you the very next day," he would threaten them. "You will be dead the moment you step out of your house." This was how he spoke to his targets.

The first attempt was made on an A-grade government contractor named Moolraj Arora. Arora introduced the flat system in Lucknow. He built Asha Apartment on the corner of Chhannilal Chauraha. It was a gated, multistoried building, the first of its kind in the city. It had a barrier at the entry, good security and a lift system. He had built Asha Apartment 1, Asha Apartment 2 and Asha Apartment 3. It was said that he had built the NER railway station in Lucknow when it was constructed, almost fifty years ago. All major central government projects landed in his kitty. He lived on the ground floor of Asha Apartment 1, a little ahead of the Sultanganj police outpost. Flats on the other floors had been sold.

Shriprakash called Moolraj Arora.

"Ashok Singh *bol raha hoon*," he boomed. "Today you went to the DRM office. There were two others with you. When you were with the DRM, there were others in the chamber. You waited for them to leave before talking to the DRM. Then you went to the clerks. You slipped 500-rupee notes into their hands."

Shriprakash narrated to him his movement of the day until he returned home and told him to pay up a sum of one crore. Moolraj Arora was unflappable. "I don't have this much money," he was curt.

Shriprakash then told him to do the math. "You sold flats for ₹25 lakh each. You even sold the parking space, making shops there for ₹20 lakh each. And you say you don't have the money."

Moolraj Arora got a little perturbed, but he kept pleading. "I don't have the money. I won't be able to give you this much."

After this, Moolraj Arora stopped taking calls; his daughter answered calls on the landline. Shriprakash called Arora two to three times. He would say he was Ashok Singh and ask for Moolraj.

"He has gone out, please call in the evening," the daughter would reply. When Moolraj didn't come on line, Shriprakash started talking indecently to the girl. He would use obscene language, the pervert that he was. This irked the daughter and she too stopped answering phones. Now a servant would pick the receiver when it rang.

Shriprakash's tricks had failed to work on Moolraj Arora. He was enraged. One morning, at around 8, he sent a message to one of his flunkeys on his pager to tell him Arora's location. The man returned the pager message at around 10.30 a.m. Moolraj Arora was sitting in his office in Saran Chamber outside Civil Hospital. Some believed that Saran Chamber 1 and Saran Chamber 2 were also built by Arora, and others said that he had bought the buildings.

Shriprakash was furious at Arora's conduct. He told Anand and Sudhir to hop into their Maruti 800 and drove off.

There was a security guard with a double-barrel gun outside the building. The three men snatched his gun, pulled him away to a corner and pointed a pistol to his head. "Take me to Arora's office," he thundered.

In Moolraj Arora's office, Shriprakash took out his AK-47 and told him to quietly walk out with them. "You think you can escape by not answering my phones. You thought I won't reach you. I need the money."

Moolraj tried to say something, but Shriprakash was not in a mood to listen to anything. He put the AK-47 back in the backpack, put a pistol on Arora's back and asked him to move out. "Don't try to act smart. Nothing will happen to us, but you will surely be dead," he whispered into his ear before Arora got to his feet.

A frightened Moolraj walked like a puppet being pulled by strings. They came out of the building, got into the car and left.

Arora was brought to a house in Viram Khand. It was a rented accommodation. A white Ambassador with a revolving red light was parked outside the building. One of Shriprakash's minions climbed over the front grille to change the light – the red light was replaced with blue light. Dhirendra Singh aka Pappu was the driver. He got at the steering wheel, Shriprakash leapt into the front seat, and Anand and Sudhir sat in the back with Moolraj Arora sandwiched between them.

The car grunted, roared and began moving.

"Bhaiyya, what if we are identified by this blue light?" Anand asked.

"Are you out of your mind?" Shriprakash said. "In India, cars with red and blue lights are never stopped or checked by the police. They would rather salute us. Cops fear if they peep inside and the officer in it identifies them. To avoid trouble, they let such cars go."

He was right. As they were approaching the police barrier ahead of Chinhat on the Lucknow–Barabanki border, the policemen posted there, lifted the barrier, gave them a salute and gestured it to go. The same thing happened in Barabanki city.

Near Faizabad, outside the Raunkahi Police Station, the police had placed drums in a zigzag manner to stop vehicles for checking. Now, the road had widened, but the checkpoint was still there. Police were as usual checking vehicles. When they saw the white Ambassador with blue light approaching, they made way for it.

The car went to Faizabad and from there directly to Mokama in Bihar.

In Mokama, Surajbhan arranged for a house for them to keep Moolraj Arora. They told Surajbhan that it was a big catch. "*Achche paise dega* (This will fetch good money)," he told Surajbhan.

Moolraj Arora kept pleading that he didn't have money and someone gave him the wrong information about him. Shriprakash would call his house in Lucknow in front of him. Mostly, the daughter answered. He would talk lecherously with her in the presence of the father. This was done to mentally break him and put him under pressure to cough up. After two or three such calls, Moolraj gave in. He said he would call his brother for the money, but they should just stop making these lewd calls. He was obviously exasperated by the dirty talks. Arora gave his brother's number to Shriprakash and a call was placed.

The brother was a senior officer in the railways and was posted in Patna. Then began the negotiations. After several rounds, they settled for fifty lakh rupees. The ransom was collected by Surajbhan's men from outside the Patna Railway Station. When the money reached Mokama, Shriprakash told Moolraj Arora that he would soon be free, but warned him to be careful with the police.

He seemed to be aware of the police-style of working. "When you reach home, they will lunge at you, subject you to innumerable rounds of questioning, won't allow you to sleep for many days. It will be a test of your nerves. Different officers will try different tricks on you and assure safety, but don't fall into their trap. They will ask you where you were taken, where you were kept, seek information about weapons used and ask if you heard train or other vehicles from where you were kept. You are a sensible man. You have seen everything. If you let out any information, some policeman will call us and tell us about it. You need to keep mum to be safe."

Shriprakash said he had asked for fifty lakh rupees and only half had been paid. "You are losing on health; you are howling and pleading with us to not call your daughter. We are letting you go, but don't forget to arrange the remaining twenty-five lakhs. You have seen how the police kept saluting us through the journey from Lucknow to Mokama. I will call you soon. Keep the money ready," he said and sent a car to drop him.

In Lucknow, Moolraj called for his car and reached home.

Like Shriprakash had said, police officers came one by one, but he had been forewarned and was mentally prepared. Police asked him where he was taken and he said Delhi. He never uttered Patna's name. The police tried different tricks, but Moolraj Arora kept thinking about arranging the rest of the money. He feared Shriprakash may harm his daughter. That fear gnawed him, and he didn't share anything worthwhile with the officers. The SSP, the SP City, along with many other officers went to his house to interrogate him, but he remained unforthcoming and cryptic.

Shriprakash called him the next day. The daughter answered. He said he was Ashok Singh and had called to find out if her father reached safely. "I will talk to you later," he said. A chill went down her back. She passed the receiver to her father.

"I know they must be sitting around you. They may even be listening to this conversation. They eavesdrop on my calls. I just called to ask if you reached safely. But don't forget your promise." Shriprakash's words echoed in Moolraj Arora's ears.

We were indeed listening to this. We found out that the call had come from Mokama. We asked him again and this time, Moolraj Arora confessed that he was taken to someplace near Patna. But he didn't give us the description of the kidnappers. We were unsure about the people who took him hostage.

About fifteen days later, Shriprakash called him again for the remaining sum of money. Moolraj only expressed his helplessness. "I have given you whatever I had and won't be able to give more." A few days passed. Shriprakash again sent for him. Moolraj was put in a car and Shriprakash announced that they were taking him away again. "You have been fooling us. Where's the money?"

"Why don't you target people with money? I don't have anything. Here you are asking me for fifty lakhs, they can give you five crore," Moolraj said. When Shriprakash asked him to suggest some such names, Moolraj named a big pharma businessman, a man who had a marble business and another one in the construction line.

Shriprakash calmed down. He said he would try to get them in ten days. If he didn't, he said, he would come back to collect the remaining amount.

Moolraj went to Delhi after a few days. Eventually, he shifted there with his family.

Chapter 6
A New SSP

Uttar Pradesh Police was under tremendous pressure. In about six months, two SSPs – Rajnikant Mishra and Subesh Kumar Singh – had been transferred out. Mishra was at the helm in Lucknow when Vivek Srivastav and Virendra Pratap Shahi were killed. Singh was the SSP when sub-inspector RK Singh was killed in a busy street of Janpath. The police had discovered that Moolraj Arora too was kidnapped by Shriprakash. When governments face pressure, they shift officers. This is still practiced. It drives home the message that the government would not brook incompetence. Newspapers write about the shunting of the officers and the public is assured that the government has acted. Both Mishra and Singh were counted among the best and had a good reputation, but they were sacrificed at the altar of governance.

In came Arun Kumar, another very bright officer.

He sat us down to understand all criminal events, from the Vivek Srivastav murder case to the abduction of Moolraj Arora. He tried to understand how gangs operated and where they operated. He asked us how much information we had collected about Shriprakash's gang. He asked us why we couldn't collect more and what the hurdles were. He asked us about the Janpath murder case and wanted to know if it could have been prevented.

He asked us about the tip-offs that we get, about our informers and how we verify the leads. Within a month and a half, he had a pretty good idea about Shriprakash's gang and its crimes. He said, let's redraw the board. We needed to handle Shriprakash soon, because his name had come to spell terror in Lucknow.

Information continued to trickle in. Some from the regular informers, some from the officers and the SSP had his own information network. Even journalists provided tip-offs. We had no other way to approach the gang, but to verify and follow these leads.

We started meeting in the police line. The chamber of RI (Reserve Inspector) was the venue. It was decided that we would meet at least twice every day, or maybe thrice. Everyone would know where we are going in the morning, meet in the afternoon to discuss updates and the evening meetings would be for planning the next day's action.

One morning, we were called urgently to the meeting room by the SSP. "Shriprakash has been seen in Lucknow," he said.

"Really? Where? He has been so cautious for the past few months," said a sub-inspector.

"It is becoming harder by the day to get information on him," added another officer.

"My informer told me that he was seen outside Mamford School in Mahanagar around 7 a.m. and then outside the Karamat Girls College. He was in his white Ambassador with revolving light outside St Fidelis, a big school in the trans-Gomti area, and near CMS in Gomti Nagar. This is happening for the past two to three days," the SSP informed us.

"This kind of information has come earlier too...," we tried to argue.

"There was no harm in checking them out. You had the information that he would come to Janpath for a shave. You went there. One day. Two days. Three days. Nothing. And then it happened," the SSP reminded us.

It was not too long ago that Moolraj Arora was kidnapped. The spectre of the incident still loomed over us. So many incidents had happened, but barring the Janpath case, in which a gang member got killed in police encounter and we recovered one AK-47 and some other weapons, our hands were empty. The government and the public were unsatisfied with such a minuscule success in Janpath. People said Shriprakash Shukla's terror was unabated. He would call people, threaten them and extort money. The newspapers were running us down in their reports every day.

The next day, during our morning briefing, SSP Arun Kumar told us that kidnapping was a shortcut for money and didn't involve much risk. Shriprakash, he said, had tasted the success of kidnapping and may be planning to kidnap a child of some rich, influential person. Someone suggested that we should find out which rich businessmen's, politician's or rich person's children studied in which school and escort them from home to school and from school to home. There were not too many buyers for this. Others said if people came to know that Shriprakash was lurking outside schools for kidnapping children, there would be bedlam in the city. No parent, rich or not, would be ready to send their children to school. We have seen whenever there's a crime against a child, every parent becomes paranoid - they fear that it could have happened to their kids too. People are extremely sensitive about their children. The officer who suggested the idea did not keep this in mind.

There was a need to monitor movements outside the schools where Shriprakash had been spotted, but this operation could bring the police department a bad name. Tevatiya, another officer working on the case, said if the information about a possible kidnapping got out in the public, schools will obviously shut down to prevent the crime, but people may say police leaked this information only to save its skin.

We didn't know how newspapers would interpret this operation. We decided to be very discreet. We had his photo and knew the two vehicles he had used. The task was divided among Satyendra Vir Singh, Avinash Mishra, who was working along with us, Tevatiya, the local police and me. I was assigned the Karamat Girls College, Satyendra Vir Singh went to the CMS, Avinash Mishra headed the team at Mamford School and Tevatiya was given the charge of St Fidelis.

It was planned that around 8 a.m., we would park ourselves at a vantage point from where we could monitor the movement of students and parents and also keep a vigil on any parked vehicles. Everyone was told to carry their wireless sets. We may hike policemen on duty, but no one would get an inkling that we were there to look for someone in particular. If people got to know that were there because of a prospective kidnapping of a child, there would be chaos. We would have a loss of face if this went out.

Everyone thought it was just a matter of half an hour or forty-five minutes. The students would settle in half an hour and school gates would be closed. We calculated that we would require being there for only this much time.

We were instructed not to react upon spotting someone who matched the description of Shriprakash or his gang members. "Inform others on the set. Force will be rushed. We will open front only when there's sufficient force," the SSP told us. We agreed because we had learnt our lessons from the Janpath incident.

We were told to meet the principals, tell them that it's a covert operation and we needed their support. If they didn't cooperate, we were told to report it to the SSP. The SSP said he would then talk to their management.

People who are aware of Lucknow would know that Karamat is in a corner in Mahanagar near the Nishatganj crossing. There's a foot over bridge near it. The college has big boundary walls and there's no room for parking outside. It has several photo studios near it and is generally a crowded area.

I had two sub-inspectors and constables each. We needed to keep an eye on the students and vehicles. We were to react if someone tried to forcibly take a kid.

I went to the principal's office. A woman around the age of thirty was the principal. I introduced myself as CO Qaisarbagh and requested her to give us some space inside the campus to monitor movement. She refused. She said it was a girls' college and she wouldn't allow any man inside. Children had begun to come inside. I told her that there were some more people with me, all policemen, and we needed to be inside the premises for some important work. She didn't budge. I called the SSP and told him about the non-cooperation. He said he was speaking to a higher-up in the management. Soon, the principal's office got a call. After speaking on the phone for some time, the principal asked about us again. I asked for some space inside the premises – an empty room, space in the staff room, some vacant place on the roof – from where we could oversee the movement outside. She said she could only allow me to be in her office.

There was a stool in her room. When I stood on the stool, I could peep outside and maintain eye contact with the other policemen. It was all right for me. When the school gate closed and we were leaving, she asked me again who I was. I said I am a deputy SP and posted as CO Qaisarbagh. She looked at the wireless and said she could overhear that the police were looking for someone. "Did that person come?" she asked.

I got annoyed. "Are you working or listening to our wireless?" I snapped at her. "This is none of your business. Don't get into this."

I was irritated and told her to talk to SSP Arun Kumar if she had any issues. I stormed out after that. She was safer not knowing too much, and so was our operation.

We got into a huddle at the police line. The SSP was briefed. Many of us had faced similar problems in schools. People were curious as well as suspicious – they wanted to find out why we were there. The SSP spoke to the management of these schools and it became smooth from the next morning.

It became a monotonous routine for us – we would go to the schools and be there until the schools began. It hadn't yielded any results so far, but we had no option.

On 13 January 1998, I was in my office and it must have been around 11 a.m. when I heard something on the set. A voice was announcing that four to five people had been shot in a white Ambassador car. I rushed to Satyendra Vir Singh's office. I told him that in the cantonment area, near the Ramnarayan petrol pump, some people had been shot. He had also heard the wireless message. We left immediately.

On the way, we got to know that four people had been killed. Four!

We heard the number "four" and went pale.

Satyendra Vir Singh said that the SSP might have been tipped that Shriprakash might be doing recce to kidnap a parent who went to drop his child. "I believe that the SSP knew that he would not be there to kidnap a child, but to do something else." Now, he had managed to commit another crime.

We had crossed the Loreto Convent and were headed towards the railway crossing.

When we were crossing Raj Bhawan Colony, there was a wail of police sirens. A lot of police vehicles with red and blue lights were whizzing past us. We called Inspector Hazratganj to find out why there was so much movement of senior police officers in that area. He told us that additional director general (ADG) CD Kainth had killed himself with his service revolver.

We reached the spot of the killings at the cantonment area. A white Ambassador with a red light on top was parked at the corner where Katai Ka Pul merges with Allahabad highway. Blood was trickling out of the car and flowing to the rain-fed nullah beside the car. The seats must have soaked some blood, and then it would have fallen on the car's floor.

We looked inside the car. It was a gory sight. Four bodies were stuck to their seats. The faces were beyond recognition. They were mere lumps of flesh. No eyes, no nose, no ears. There was flesh on the car roof. One of them was in police uniform. The car bore a red board in the front – Upadhyaksh, Uttar Pradesh Cooperative Bank Limited.

Upendra Vikram Singh had been killed. He was a sturdy man wearing white kurta-pajama, which had now turned completely red.

The SSP also arrived. We found out that the fourth man was some Shukla, a big contractor from Allahabad. They were headed for Allahabad from the bank headquarters.

Satyendra Vir Singh took me aside and whispered in my ears, "Do you have any doubt?" I whimpered, "No."

There is no habitation near the place. The petrol pump is also a little away. There are some pan shops near the railway crossing. We went to one of them and asked about the incident. The man had witnessed the entire incident.

The man said he saw a white Maruti 800 come and park with its face towards Loreto Convent School. Two men came out of it, one from the driving seat, and the other from behind. Then there was this white Ambassador coming down from Katai Ka Pul. When the car drove closer, the man from the driving seat of the parked Maruti 800 picked up a big weapon and shot the driver and gunner in the front; the other man whipped out two pistols from his trousers and shot the two men in the back seat.

He said he had often heard the boom of weapons during firing practice in the military area close by and the weapon seemed one of those because the gunfire was very loud. We showed him our gunner's AK-47 and he immediately identified it to be the same weapon.

The man put the AK-47 back in the car and shot the men in the back seat with his pistol, three bullets each. A Tata Sumo was coming from behind. It had a rifle, which was visible from a distance. This man flashed the AK-47 and ran towards it. The Tata Sumo reversed and sped off in the direction from which it was coming.

None of us had any doubt about who could have been behind this killing.

We came straight to the SSP's office. The area where the killing occurred fell under the jurisdiction of Hazratganj. My counterpart also came. The SSP spoke to them. Then he called us, the team working on Shriprakash Shukla.

We said the cartridges found were from a .45mm pistol. .45 is a weapon used by the American Army. During the British time, the weapon was used to kill elephants. It seemed that the same weapon was used to shoot the faces of the dead men.

The police didn't have any doubt about whose handiwork this was. Hundreds of bullets had been fired, an AK-47 had been used and the murder was committed despite the presence of several red and blue light-fitted cars barely a hundred metres away.

The chutzpah left nothing for us to guess.

The newspapers wrote different versions of the incident the next day, based on conjectures, some of which were contradictory. A VIP with a policeman had been killed in a white Ambassador car fitted with red light. No wonder the incident had political repercussions. Pressure on the police was mounting.

We were almost certain about who was behind this, but newspaper reporters were blaming different gangs for the killings. Some said Sattu Pandey had done it, and others wrote of the involvement of Laddu Singh gang of Banaras. There were some more suspects in news reports.

Shriprakash suffered from *chhapas rog*, a colloquial word for people who are hungry for publicity. He also wanted the newspapers to write about his exploits.

His network of people from Gorakhpur and surrounding areas, whom he had developed and nurtured over the years, was more than willing to help him. He had spotted their talent. They read all the newspapers in the morning and briefed Shriprakash when he wanted to know about any coverage. A message would be dropped on someone's pager to call Bhaiyya from a particular PCO. They would tell him about the coverage in that day's newspaper.

A couple of days after Upendra Vikram Singh's murder, Shriprakash found out through news reports that some reporters were unsure about who was behind the killings. Some newspapers had indeed hinted that it could only have been Shriprakash because of the weapons used and the number of bullets fired, but no one was categorical about him.

Upendra Vikram Singh himself didn't have a clean history. He had several adversaries. So people tended to believe that it could have been some other gang too. Shriprakash called a correspondent of a reputed newspaper and asked him about the source of his information. He warned him to not misreport otherwise he may be in trouble. "I am Shriprakash, and I killed that man," he announced.

The correspondent got scared. He contacted SSP Arun Kumar and told him about the phone call. He didn't have a recording facility so couldn't record the call. The number was shared with us and we traced it to a PCO in Nepalganj town of Nepal. The correspondent, meanwhile, stopped writing names of other gangs in his newspaper, but still withheld from mentioning Shriprakash's name unequivocally.

Newspapers started questioning our competence. They wrote that the police weren't doing anything despite such big criminal activities. They haven't been able to break this gang, they wrote. Police failure was being highlighted in newspapers almost every day. Senior officers also read the papers and got influenced. This began reflecting in the meetings.

One day,.SSP Arun Kumar called all of us to his office. When we entered his office, we found him to be deep in thought. He gestured us to take our seats. "See, I was telling you that he is here. Our information was right. We can't say for sure that he had committed these murders, but more or less it looks like him," he said.

"We are doing our best. All teams were monitoring schools. We were anticipating another kidnapping but didn't know that he had other plans," I said.

"Do we have any fresh clue?"

"We have got hold of a car, some documents and some pamphlets. Apart from that, we haven't got anything," replied Satyendra Vir Singh.

The SSP was lost in worry and stared outside the window into oblivion.

On 8 November 1997, Vivek Ladhani, son of Cola-Cola bottling plant owner Laxman Das Ladhani, was returning home from work in the evening when a red Esteem car overtook him. Three men got out of the car, pulled Vivek out of his car, dragged him into their car, fired three times in the air and took him away. Within a few hours, the father got a ransom call. The caller demanded five crore rupees and identified himself as Shriprakash Shukla. The Ladhanis had the biggest bottling business in North India at that time.

So a kidnapping did happen! We began working on old information that we had. One team was permanently in Gorakhpur. One team was going to Bihar too. Meanwhile, Vivek was taken to Delhi and kept in a flat. The family kept negotiating with the kidnappers and they settled for one crore rupees. The ransom was paid and Vivek returned home.

By now, we had become more familiar with mobile phone technology. Shriprakash's gang had started using mobile phones more. We would work on CDRs and find out about the locations of numbers appearing on those bulky printouts. A lot of landlines featured on the CDRs - some of them were of Shriprakash's victims, and some of them were of his aides.

Everyone was concerned about his rising terror. In regular meetings at the DG office, we felt pressure from senior police officers and the government. There had been two big kidnappings in Lucknow. Both from busy marketplaces.

We resolved that we won't allow any more kidnappings. But because there was no other information that we could work on, we thought we may have a chance encounter with him like in Janpath and narrowed down his possible targets. Meanwhile, the vigil outside schools where children of big businessmen studied continued.

I went back to Karamat again. When school management or a teacher allows you to use their space for two hours without knowing your purpose, they often get curious. They try different ways to find out. When I returned to Karamat after so many days, the principal, Saima Khalid, said she could help us if we told her our purpose. But we had to guard the secret with our lives.

This routine continued for many days and then on 12 November, Arun Kumar also got transferred. Since Shriprakash entered the Lucknow underworld, three SSPs had been changed, to quote the newspapers, for their failure to rein in the dreaded criminal.

All three – Rajnikant Mishra, Subesh Kumar Singh and Arun Kumar – were outstanding officers, not just in UP but in the entire police fraternity. But still, they were removed after their short tenures.

We felt demotivated. Arun Kumar was a hard taskmaster. He seemed to be on the right track to take this campaign forward. He had developed very important information. It was unfortunate that we couldn't achieve success. After his transfer, there came a time when we thought it was impossible to neutralise this gangster.

With time, Shriprakash had become more wayward. He was threatening even the cabinet ministers. The then election commissioner also got a threat call from him. The government thought it had had enough and couldn't take it anymore. Ajay Raj Sharma, who had been ADG Law and Order, but had since moved out, was called by the then chief minister Kalyan Singh.

We got to know about this later from a book that Ajay Raj Sharma had penned. Otherwise, we wouldn't have known about this conversation between the two of them. The CM had mentioned that Shriprakash has crossed all limits; he has started talking about eliminating even the chief minister. This was very grave. The CM told Ajay Raj Sharma to take charge of ADG Law and Order again the next day.

Ajay Raj Sharma agreed to accept the mantle only on the condition that he would be given a free hand to put together a team. He had been in the UP Police for a long time and knew all the officers who were truly passionate about policing and investigations. That would help him keep the fluff – people who only have stories to narrate and did no real work – out of this very special operation. He told the CM that if he would be allowed to put together this specialised team, he would surely get the criminal.

Kalyan Singh gave him the green light. "You are free to choose your team, but this has to end now. We cannot allow any more murders in the city." The CM was famous for his strictness. He had zero tolerance for crimes and criminals. Such big crimes during his tenure as the CM seemed a blot on his reputation. After getting out of the CM's office, Ajay Raj Sharma called a few people to join his team.

Arun Kumar was the first to be contacted. He was told to suggest people who had worked on the cases with him. Ajay Raj Sharma said the government wanted to form a special unit that will work only on Shriprakash Shukla. He told Arun Kumar to have a word with people in his team. "If they are willing to be a part of this special unit, get an undertaking from them," he told Arun Kumar.

I remember, it must have been April or May. It was a typical humid, sultry day when Arun Kumar drove to Satyendra Vir Singh's office in his personal car. I was also called to the office of the SP City. It was very hot; all of us were sweating. If I remember correctly, there was a power outage. Arun Kumar told us that Ajay Raj Sharma would probably return in a day or two as ADG Law and Order and he has been tasked with creating a special unit to end Shriprakash's terror. He told us that the government wanted a small team of maybe just ten-odd people.

We had our reservations. Where would its office be located? Who would we report to? Would we be part of the district police or not? We lobbed some of these tricky yet vital questions at Arun Kumar. He had some answers, but was equally clueless about the details. He said it would not be possible for him to arrange and work with a new team. That was why he was keen to have people who had already worked on the Shriprakash case with him.

"They may get their feet wet," he said. "You know how people work; they would talk pompously, but if they are required to go on an operation, they become nervous."

Satyendra Vir Singh and I said yes to the proposal. Arun Kumar took a paper and wrote an application addressing the DG on our behalf, expressing our willingness to be part of the special team. We both signed the application. We thought since all big crimes had occurred in the area under our jurisdiction, we could only take any effective action against Shriprakash if we got on the team. Otherwise, people would continue to believe that Shriprakash had outsmarted us.

Arun Kumar left with the application. He said the order would be out soon. We told him again to have a separate set-up for the unit and have different office and telephone connections.

Four days later, the government issued an order relieving Satyendra Vir Singh from the post of SP City, me of the duties of CO Qaisarbagh and posting us to a new unit which was nameless. The district police have their own SOGs (Special Operations Groups). People said this was the DG's own SOG.

We started looking for an office. The government allotted us one room in the DG office, but Arun Kumar declined the offer. He said all senior officers sit there. They have visitors. We won't be able to work independently from there. He asked for a space outside the police set-up. He also asked for the safety of the team.

Our government vehicles were withdrawn, the landline connections were disconnected and our followers were withdrawn. The ADG LO was requested for a vehicle from the DG pool. We got one Ambassador but it would become unavailable if there was a senior officer from another state, former DGs or officers from agencies like the CBI in town. On those days, we used Satyendra Vir Singh's Maruti 800. We were scouting for a place and were also looking out for more talent from the police to join our team.

This was the time when OP Tripathi, Malviya and Satyendra Tripathi came on board. The ADG LO said, "This is going to be a top-secret operation. Only people who are part of the operation will know about it." For secrecy, the operation was code-named Operation Bazooka. "Bazooka is an uncommon word. Even if someone overheard our conversation related to this operation, they would be unable to guess that this is an operation against Shriprakash Shukla," the ADG added. "We cannot afford to let anyone track our moves on this operation."

For the office, we identified some houses, but whenever people used to find out that we were police officers, they would back out. Some would say it wasn't vacant and others would talk about consulting their brothers or children. But we knew that these were excuses. The fact was they were cagey about renting their properties to the police.

Meanwhile, the gazette notification for the formation of a Special Task Force was issued.

Chapter 7
The Wrestler from Mamkhor

Ram Samujh Shukla was a teacher at a government school in Mamkhor village in Gorakhpur. His wife, Shanti Devi, was a homemaker and looked after their five children - four sons, Omprakash, Girish, Chandraprakash and Shriprakash, and a daughter, Sunita. Like his elder brothers, Shriprakash, born in 1972, loved wrestling in the village *akhara.* He had a toned body and an upturned nose. Shriprakash studied in the village government school till the tenth standard and then moved to Gorakhpur for senior secondary. He lived in Pathar Kothi in Daudpur mohalla under the Cantonment Police Station. The wrestler from Mamkhor soon got into bad company and graduated from a science student of a secondary school to a history-sheeter of the Cantonment Police Station. The lure of the gun consumed this young man in his teens and by the time he was twenty-one, he had already committed one murder.

He committed his first murder in 1993 - the story goes that someone harassed his sister and he killed him. But the fact was that Shriprakash had arguments with one Rakesh Tiwari over harassment of other girls in the mohalla and Shriprakash bludgeoned him to death. The fight for dominance took an ugly turn, and because Shriprakash had a wrestler's body, Tiwari couldn't take the attack.

The murder made Shriprakash a dreaded man in the locality. A small-time goon of Daudpur, Bablu Tiwari, introduced

Shriprakash to Anand Pandey and Satyavrat Rai. Anand belonged to Jorwa Mehendawal of Sant Kabirnagar district. Satyavrat was from Belabujarg village under Sikriganj Police Station of Gorakhpur. The two lived in Hydel Colony under Cantonment Police Station and had been together in MP College. They lusted after money and had taken to crime. They believed in the dictum that gun power could get one plenty of money.

The cable television business had started in India in 1994. Operators provided satellite TV to subscribers along with a cable network for a subscription fee of hundred rupees, which was collected at the end of every month. Fee collection was a tricky affair as people would often refuse to pay even at the cost of disconnection. For the lack of staff, operators were unable to collect fees every month and would often go to collect the pending fees at the end of several months. Operators employed small-time goons and local musclemen as collection agents and paid them hefty commissions. Between the first and seventh of every month, these goons went from door to door, collecting subscription charges. People dreaded them and paid up to avoid trouble. The commission, which was as high as forty percent of the total collection, amounted to big money and it cost the ruffians nothing to earn it. The operators were content with the remaining sixty percent.

Anand Pandey and Satyavrat Rai found it a lucrative business. They could easily make fifteen to twenty thousand rupees per month – which was a huge sum of money in the early 1990s –

without actually doing anything. They thought they would gradually expand the business. Thinking that this was the easiest way to make big money in a very short time, the two dived headlong into the business. Someone called Raja Gupta was already in the cable business. He obviously didn't like competition from these new players. But Anand Pandey and Satyavrat Rai were *gundas*, who proved to be more powerful than Raja Gupta's goons. The two were usurping Gupta's customers and this led to acrimony between the two groups. The staff of the rival operators often had fights.

One day, when Raja was sitting at a tea stall, Anand shot him. Fortunately, Raja survived. Anand was booked for an attempt to murder under section 307 of the IPC. This failed attempt made Anand and Satyavrat realize that they needed more powerful men with them to rule the business – or even survive it. Shriprakash already had a murder to his name. They lured him into the business. Their proposition was lucrative – if Shriprakash came onboard, they could expand themselves from two to three mohallas to the whole of Gorakhpur. The money that they would make in a year would help them start something bigger and better.

Raja Gupta was not the only hurdle. There were four more names famous in the cable business in their part of the city. Niraj Singh, Sona Tiwari, Deepak Agarwal and Hriday Chand had their own areas, but all of them were looking for opportunities to expand. There was Anand, Satyavrat and Shriprakash on the one hand and these already established players on the other. All of them were looking for grounds to make more money. Clashes were eminent.

One day, Niraj Singh shot Hriday Chand dead. After this, Sona Tiwari and Deepak Agrawal murdered Niraj Singh, who was also Shriprakash's friend. They had some understanding. Niraj Singh and Hriday Chand were big players in the cable business. Their deaths left a vacuum that had to be filled. Sona Tiwari and Deepak Agrawal weren't big enough. So, they all came together and decided to work together to prevent the entry of a third party, who would benefit from their rivalry.

Anand, Satyavrat, Shriprakash, Sona and Deepak got control of the cable business of almost half the city. The other half was still in charge of two other players - Anshuman Singh and Dubey. The five decided to eliminate the two to become the undisputed cable gang of the city. Shriprakash and Anand killed Anshuman Singh and Dubey in a matter of one month. The group now had a carbine that they got from Dubey after killing him. They were unabashed as their firepower increased.

In 1996, Arun Mishra, a corporator, was killed in Gorakhpur. Shriprakash had good relations with the politician. He learnt that someone called Gyan Srivastav was behind this. Shriprakash attacked Gyan Srivastav to take revenge. However, Srivastav's father was killed in the attack. After that, the trio of Shriprakash, Anand and Satyavrat committed more than twenty murders in and around Gorakhpur. They became uninhibited and would kill people on the street in broad daylight without an ounce of fear.

Shriprakash had arrived at the crime scene. But for him to become the trigger-happy crime lord that he eventually became, he needed weapons and the support of a big mafia gang. Surajbhan Singh of Bihar was a ganglord. He had been trying to grab meaty railway contracts for years. Surajbhan had heard stories of the bravado of Shriprakash and his gang. The man, a bit of a madcap, was only twenty-four in 1996 when he already had about twenty murders on his hands. Shriprakash, Surajbhan learnt, harboured the ambition of becoming India's top gangster and yearned for an AK-47.

At that time, Shriprakash used to travel in a Maruti Gypsy, an open mini-truck, which was looted from the brother-in-law of a former Meghalaya politician, who had been a minister in 1995. The vehicle was looted after the murder of the brother-in-law in Kuchaikote of Gopalganj district. The Gypsy had a red light atop it. When Shriprakash drove, Anand would sit in the front seat with the carbine. It seemed as if the Gypsy was a government vehicle and the man in the front seat was a police guard. Shriprakash used this vehicle in most of his operations.

On 5 September 1994, after Surajbhan Singh's ally Chhutkun Shukla was slain by his gunner Ajay Singh, there was a major protest in Muzaffarpur, Bihar. Chhutkun's brothers, Butkun and Munna, were part of the crowd demonstrating against the killing the next day. Gopalganj's district magistrate (DM) was on his way to Patna from Muzaffarpur for a meeting. The mob stopped him, surrounded his official vehicle and eventually killed him. A serving DM had not only been lynched, but also killed. This didn't go down well with the police, who began raiding places in search of the protesters.

The Shukla brothers were growing impatient. They wanted to take revenge for their brother's murder. They got in touch with Surajbhan. Surajbhan roped in Shriprakash for a contract killing.

He had heard that these young men from Gorakhpur were daring and could go to any length. Shriprakash was put in touch with the Shukla brothers. "Our rivals flushed Ajay Singh with money to buy his loyalty. We can pay you any amount to eliminate him. He deserves the same type of death," Butkun told Shriprakash in their first meeting. Along with Anand Pandey and Sudhir Tripathi, the three agreed to take the contract for killing Ajay Singh.

They were told that Ajay Singh would be brought to court with tight police security. Shriprakash was not to be daunted by weapons.

"It doesn't matter how many weapons you have," he said. "*Jiski goli pehle lag jayegi wahi badshah hai, wahi badmash hai* (the person who fires the first bullet is the king)," he told Surajbhan, assuring him that Ajay Singh would be dead.

Shriprakash, Anand and Sudhir went to Gopalganj with two of Surajbhan's men for local support. They found out about the next court hearing and set up an ambush.

On the day of the trial, Ajay Singh got off the police van with three policemen flanking either side of him. There was a huge commotion of both common people and the media. His face was covered in black cloth. Shriprakash and gang came on motorbikes and shot Ajay Singh without even getting off. Four policemen were injured too. Ajay Singh's body was pierced with twenty-one bullets. Ajay Singh was killed in judicial custody.

The gang returned to Mokama and went straight to Surajbhan. He was very happy. He said the three had indeed displayed a courageous act.

"Butkun and Munna are also capable, but they didn't dare to take revenge for their brother's death," Surajbhan said, to make the operation sound even more important.

Shriprakash used to call Surajbhan *dada.* He said, "Dada, we need an AK-47."

Surajbhan had a cache of AK-47s. The story of how he acquired the arms is no less interesting than Shriprakash's exploits and crimes. During the Purulia arms drop case in 1995, when a foreign plane had dropped weapons, which were later recovered from parts of Bihar and West Bengal, Surajbhan found out that some of them were dropped in a pond. The water body was searched and fourteen AK-47s were recovered. The gang kidnapped the armourer of the CRPF camp and brought him to Mokama. The armourer was in Surajbhan's custody for a month. He had to clean the rust from the sophisticated weapons and make them functional. He was eventually released after this work was accomplished.

Surajbhan gave one Kalashnikov assault rifle to Shriprakash from this tranche. It was recovered after an encounter.

Criminals in Bihar kept Surajbhan in good humour because of these AK-47s; they banked on him for help with the weapon when needed. Shriprakash was also aware of this and asked for an AK-47. Surajbhan promised him one, but only after Shriprakash would eliminate some more of his enemies. Surajbhan had made this offer earlier too. When they went to attack Shahi at Gol Ghar in Gorakhpur, he had promised two AK-47s to Shriprakash if he killed Shahi. However, Shahi survived the attack and the arms never came to Shriprakash. They got two of these guns after they killed Shahi in Lucknow later in January 1997; one was taken by Shriprakash, while Anand kept the other one.

Shriprakash was fond of weapons and kept pleading Surajbhan for more AK-47s. Surajbhan would use Shriprakash to eliminate his adversaries in return for the promise of more weapons.

Surajbhan got Manoj Singh, Vijay Singh and Ajay Singh killed by Shriprakash, Anand and Sudhir. It created a sensation in Patna. They were one of the biggest contractors in Patna in 1997. Their killing left the entire town in horror. The FIR mentioned the assailant shouting *Jai Bajrang Bali* after shooting the three dead. It is said that Shriprakash would let out this victory cry after every murder, a fact mentioned in the FIRs.

When they went back to Mokama, Surajbhan said, "You deserve one more AK. Take it from me before you leave Mokama." Shriprakash could see his dream coming true.

Meanwhile, Surajbhan had another enemy who needed to be fixed. Shriprakash offered his help in killing him too while they were in Mokama, but Surajbhan discouraged him. "There's too much noise about the three murders and it may not be safe for you to go to Patna. If you get identified, you may get into trouble. That will be a big problem for me too," Surajbhan said.

He continued, "Although it's a difficult job, I need to eliminate this nuisance within a week, before the next tender." Three more men had come to him from Gorakhpur. One of them was called Gandhi. Surajbhan said, "These men are also good. I will give the next assignment to these new ones."

Shriprakash didn't want someone else to work for Surajbhan. He said he won't be identified and requested Surajbhan to let him do the work, but Surajbhan insisted that Shriprakash should not get himself involved further.

"Let me try them; if they fail, I will allow you," he said.

Lallan Singh, son of Surajbhan's uncle Ram Balak Singh, was sent with Gandhi's gang to identify the target, with a clear instruction that the man has to be killed that day itself. They went to Patna, chased the target through the day and in the evening, when he was near Gandhi Maidan, they killed him. They overtook his vehicle and rained bullets on him. The man also had two sophisticated weapons in the car, but Gandhi and the group didn't allow him time to use them.

They brought the weapons recovered from the target's car with them when they returned to Surajbhan. He was ecstatic. "*Gorakhpur ke paani me hi kuch aisa hai* (There is something in Gorakhpur's water)," he was brimming with happiness. The three had killed the man within seconds. Surajbhan said the precision of the operation proved that they were good. Shriprakash, Anand and Sudhir were also there when Surajbhan was singing paeans for the new group.

Shriprakash didn't enjoy Surajbhan praising someone else in his presence. These people could become his rivals in the future, he thought to himself.

After dinner, they left for the nearby mosque where Surajbhan and the gangs were putting up. Surajbhan had several houses in Mokama. He would often send Shriprakash to one in which his elderly sister lived. But that day, they all were to sleep in the mosque.

The two groups didn't talk to each other during dinner. In the mosque, Gandhi said he and his friends would sleep on the rooftop. Shriprakash rejected this idea, saying, "You should have asked dada if you wanted to go to the rooftop."

Gandhi said dada won't say anything and went upstairs with the bedding. His two aides followed suit.

In the room, Shriprakash became restless. Sleep eluded him. Sudhir sensed the cause of Shriprakash's anxiety and reassured, "Bhaiyya, you are over thinking. These buggers can't match us."

Shriprakash poured out his insecurity. "I think dada deliberately didn't allow us to go to Patna today. *Hamari cutting kar rahe hain* (He's cutting us off). Didn't you notice how he was showering praise on them for this small work?"

Anand Pandey also woke up. "We have no choice. We need to take three to four AK-47s from him. No gang in UP has so many AK-47s. This is a war of domination and we need weapons for this. If we have that many AK-47s, we can take on even the Army, let alone the police. We need to create a space for us in the system, get into it and then graduate to full-time politics," he said rather prophetically.

The discussion ended and they went back to sleep, but Shriprakash did not sleep a wink. Around 3 a.m., he nudged the other two awake and said, "Let's go upstairs."

Anand and Sudhir objected to this, but Shriprakash was adamant. They had a .45mm pistol, an AK-47 and a .9mm pistol. Other weapons were in the bag. They went upstairs and found the three sleeping on the floor of the rooftop. Gandhi and his gang had worked the whole day and drank in the evening. They were sleeping like logs.

"I will shoot Gandhi on the head and you fire five bullets each on the other two," Shriprakash announced.

Fifteen bullets punctured the silence of the night in the sleepy town. Shriprakash got nervous. He thought that Surajbhan or his men may rush after hearing gunshots and they may land in trouble. So he decided to sit there for fifteen to twenty minutes.

No one came. There was too much blood on the rooftop. Shriprakash suggested that the bodies should be dumped in the Ganga, which flew barely a hundred steps from the mosque.

"I don't know how dada will react to this because he had become fond of them. We need to dispose of the bodies before he finds out," Shriprakash said. The other two got cold feet. But they anyway lend him their help when he picked one body on his shoulder and began to climb down the stairs.

They walked through the sand and went to the *ghat*. A few boats were anchored there. They unroped one of them and dumped the three corpses on it. The boat was oared to the middle of the river and the bodies were thrown into the flowing river.

They returned to the riverbank, cleaned the blood from the boat and came to take the blood-soaked bedding. A second boat was used to take the mattresses and bed sheets to the river.

On their way back, they encountered a gang member of Surajbhan. "*Ashok bhai, aap jahan ruke the, waha goli chali thi kya* (Was there firing at the place where you are put up)?" he inquired.

Shriprakash was known as Ashok Singh in Mokama. Surajbhan also called him by that name. He didn't want any of his men to know his real name. This was a strategy to save him from the police if he ever got caught.

"No," Shriprakash said without batting an eyelid. "We were unable to sleep so went to the river for a stroll. When we were in the boat, we fired in the air. You may have heard that," he replied.

"You shouldn't have done it," he said. "This is Mokama. You don't know the gang rivalries here. Dada sent me to find out. You should be careful."

The three returned to the rooftop. They brought buckets of water from the first floor to wash the blood off the floor.

"*Tumne theek nahi kiya* (You shouldn't have done this)," Surajbhan said at the dining table when they went to his house for breakfast the next morning.

Shriprakash feigned ignorance. Surajbhan said that in Mokama, even mosquitoes and flies need my permission to fly. Shriprakash remained silent. "Gandhi and his men were a daring lot. They worked for us. My work and your work are no different. There was no need to kill them," Surajbhan sounded annoyed.

Shriprakash offered to explain. "They were talking through their hat in front of you, but they were greedy. Tomorrow someone may give them more money and turn them against you. We are your trusted people. They were untrustworthy."

But Surajbhan didn't buy this argument. The meeting ended abruptly.

When they returned to their room, Shriprakash said, "Dada seemed to be in a foul mood. It is better to leave Mokama at the earliest." Anand and Sudhir had participated in the last night's violence half-heartedly. They said with trepidation, "We cannot leave Mokama without his permission."

During dinner, Shriprakash told Surajbhan that there was a wedding in his family and he wanted to go to Gorakhpur.

Surajbhan suggested against this. "There's pressure from UP Police and Bihar Police. The needle of suspicion for the four murders is on me. I've recently started working in politics. If you are caught, my career will fall before it can take off," he said.

"Okay, then we won't go to Gorakhpur. We will go to Nepal. You may put in a word to Pappu Dev in Viratnagar for us. He will organize our stay there. We will be there for two weeks. The police will become lax in the meantime," Shriprakash said.

Obviously, Surajbhan understood the police better. He began talking like an elderly person. "First of all, it was a blunder to kill a police officer. When a policeman is killed, the police of all states become one. Don't be under the misconception that they won't be chasing you. Don't go to Gorakhpur or Lucknow even by mistake."

Shriprakash was ready to take all advice; he wanted to get out of Mokama as soon as possible. "Dada, you are right. I will go directly to Nepal," he reiterated.

The next morning, around 4 a.m., Anand, Sudhir and Shriprakash left Patna for Viratnagar. They called Pappu Dev en route and told him to make arrangements for them.

The bodies of Gandhi and the two others were never found.

When we were working on the Shriprakash cases, we thought of seeking the help of families of Gandhi and his aides killed by Shriprakash. We met them in Gorakhpur. They hadn't performed the last rites. "We never found the bodies," they told us. They said they were sure that the three had been killed and suspected Shriprakash's role in it, but they had no proof.

Fast forward to 1997... When people heard that Shriprakash had become a menace in UP, they started providing information to the three SSPs of Lucknow - Rajnikant Mishra, Subesh Kumar Singh and Arun Kumar - as and when they held office. They are the ones who bore the brunt of that gangsters' exploits.

We had been hearing about his activities in Mokama, but we needed to establish it. It was thought difficult, rather impossible, to plant a man in Mokama to get information about Shriprakash. Only the locals could help. Someone offered to get us the number that Surajbhan used. We could get in touch with Shriprakash through this number, the informer said, but it had to be someone known to Surajbhan or Lallan Singh, who mostly answered the call. Surajbhan didn't talk to strangers.

From the call that we had intercepted, we knew that Shriprakash spoke in chaste Bhojpuri and was very abusive. Even when he spoke in Hindi to his targets, he had a distinct Bhojpuri accent. None of us - Satyendra Vir Singh, Avinash Mishra, Tevatiya or I - were from eastern UP. I was from Allahabad and our family spoke Hindi. But my maternal grandparents and my in-laws were from a Bhojpuri-speaking area. Shriprakash used some words which were difficult to decipher.

The SSP suggested that if we were to talk to him to confirm his presence in Mokama, one of us needed to speak his language. "We have heard him in telephone recordings. If we hear him and establish that he is there, we can raid Mokama with the help of Patna police and take effective action against him," the SSP said.

We would often be visiting towns like Banaras or Gorakhpur in eastern UP following his telephone locations. On the way to Banaras, we would stop for tea breaks at Pratap Dhaba on the Faizabad bypass in Sultanpur. It was located midway between Lucknow and Banaras. At the corner of the dhaba was a kiosk that often played Bhojpuri songs by Manoj Tiwari. The songs were pleasant and melodious.

This was 1997. Manoj Tiwari was only a singer. He had made a distinct place for himself in the Bhojpuri music industry because his songs were bereft of the obscenities associated with Bhojpuri songs, especially those by Baleshwar. You could listen to Manoj Tiwari's songs with family.

I would pick cassettes of Manoj Tiwari from that shop. The purpose was to familiarize myself with the language and pick up peculiar words in common use so that we could understand the conversations and even speak the language if and when needed. I would play those cassettes in our official cars. Sometimes Satyendra Vir would get irritated and say, "I don't know what is wrong with you."

He was from western UP and these songs were obviously not music to his ears. His driver would sometimes play songs from western UP to settle the score.

One day, the SSP enquired if I would be able to talk to Shriprakash.

Before I could reply, Satyendra Vir Singh interposed, "Why not, sir! He listens to Bhojpuri songs all day."

I said I could try. "Won't I sound amateur?" I said, adding, "I won't be able to talk for long. If he is smart, the person on the other end can easily make out that Bhojpuri is not my native language."

About fifteen days later, everyone was called to the SSP's office and told that Shriprakash was in Mokama.

"Here are the three numbers that Surajbhan or his men use. We need to call them to find out if Shriprakash is still there," the SSP said, passing a chit of paper to us. The numbers were scribbled with a red pen.

How would we get him on the line? Everyone began thinking. It was said that there's a block *pramukh* named JP Singh who was close to Shriprakash. He was in jail for his connection to the Virendra Shahi murder case. He passed on information about people to Shriprakash. He had either been released on bail or was about to.

I was tasked with the job of collecting information about him.

"Rajesh, you talk to Shriprakash, posing as JP Singh," the SSP told me. "Say that you are the block pramukh from Gorakhpur and that you want to speak to Ashok Singh. He would immediately come on line on hearing the name of JP Singh, because he would be clueless about his release."

The office phones were not to be used to make the call. The officers said criminals always keep a list of police telephone numbers and that could expose us. "Gangs keep a record of landline numbers of important offices, such as that of the SSP or SP City in their diary," someone said. We decided to use a PCO. I said I won't go alone. I wanted the team to come with me.

There were five to six PCOs in a row in Qaisarbagh in front of the office of the SP City. An inspector from the team vacated one of the PCOs. The operator was asked not to allow anyone in while we were there. Even otherwise, people were unlikely to walk into a PCO surrounded by the police.

We dialled the number. Someone answered.

"Hello, *kaun* (who)?" The man said.

"I am JP Singh from Gorakhpur. Please put me through to Ashok bhaiyya, it's urgent," I said.

"JP Singh, who?" he asked.

"Block pramukh JP Singh," I answered.

"Ok. Call after half an hour."

We waited in the PCO. After half an hour, the number was redialled. The same person answered.

"JP Singh?"

"Ji, JP Singh."

"Here, talk to Ashok Singh."

Shriprakash was on the line. "Did you get bail?" he asked.

"Yes, I got it," I said.

"But Muktinath Mishra said bail was difficult this time. He will try it on the next date," he said after a brief pause.

"I came for the court appearance," I said, "and thought of updating you."

He hung up.

Probably he got suspicious. He had updates about JP Singh. We were wrong to assume that he may not be aware of the developments and we could spook him. He had spoken to Muktinath Mishra, his lawyer, a few days earlier.

Our plan to engage him on phone went kaput.

But we had the confirmation that he was in Mokama and that he was in touch with Surajbhan. This was vital. Satyendra Vir Singh told the SSP about the conversation. He said Shriprakash was either in Surajbhan's house or at a place arranged by Surajbhan.

The SSP said it was good news. "Let me speak to the CM. If a state plane can be arranged, you guys can then leave for Patna right away," he said. "I will speak to SSP Patna. He will organize things for you."

It was around four in the evening. A state plane was arranged. We rushed home to pack clothes and came to Amausi Airport. The weapons – five AK-47s, pistols, revolvers and cartridges – were put on the plane.

We were told that someone called Murari Lal Meena, the SP RA (Rural Area), would assist us in Bihar. "Don't get in touch with anyone else. He will organize a raid," the SSP told us before the plane took off.

SSP Patna had ostensibly told SSP Lucknow that Mokama was two and a half hours from Patna and it was a difficult area due to its congested lanes. But he promised to organize the raid the same day.

Chapter 8
The Failed Raid

At the airport in Patna, police vehicles came to receive us. We drove straight to the office of the SP RA. An ASP was also present there. We briefed the SP about the big crimes committed by Shriprakash and his gang, especially the murder of sub-inspector RK Singh. We said we knew he was in Mokama, and also let him know about how we had tracked him down.

It was nearly sunset when we reached the office of SP RA. He informed that Mokama gets completely deserted after 6 p.m. There are several gangs in Mokama and they are always at loggerheads with each other. "If you go now, the operation may not be successful. News about a police party may spread before your arrival and you won't find anything," he said.

It made sense. We decided to go by his plan. The SP said that we should wait until the next morning.

"Let me organize our intelligence on the ground for the night. We have some links in the groups who are rivals of Surajbhan. They will let us know about his exact location. You can start around four in the morning so that you can reach there before dawn," he said.

"Early morning raids are always successful," the SP added.

We left Patna for Mokama at around 4 a.m. in police and private vehicles. The ASP and a deputy SP were also with us. It was decided in the previous evening's meeting that the Mokama police would not be informed about the operation. "We will not involve them in this," the SP had said.

On the way, the ASP told us that they suspected Mokama inspector's integrity and thus decided to not even take the help of the local police.

The cavalcade was moving with headlights turned off. We entered Mokama town and were surprised to find men atop houses. There was a man on top of every fourth house. A man came to our help. Meena Sir must have organized this.

"Do you get there so early in the morning?" we wondered aloud to him. He told us about the gangs there. "Everyone keeps an eye on everyone here. By now, everyone in Mokama must have got the information about the police," he said, to impress upon us about how fast information travels in that sleepy town.

We were ten minutes away from the house we were heading to. The ASP had another of his men on the ground. He signalled to us to get down from the vehicle and enter a lane.

As we were walking to the house, we saw it parked right before our eyes outside the house – the white Ambassador. This was the car that the gang had used in all the kidnappings.

The house had a small front. The door was ajar. We walked in with loaded guns in our hands. The gang also had AK-47s and the house was Surajbhan's den. Nothing could be left to chance.

We got in gingerly. We didn't find anything in the first room. In the second room, we found three unzipped big bags. They were good-quality airbags. There were also three pairs of shoes. Toothbrushes were strewn on the bed.

It seemed the men had escaped barely five minutes ago.

The bags were searched. We found RK Singh's pistol and recovered the key of the Ambassador. They didn't get time to pack the AK-47 that Shriprakash's gang normally used to carry around in a cricket bag.

We went upstairs, to the first floor, where we found an elderly woman. We asked her about the people who were in the house and had left before our arrival. She was reluctant to answer any of our questions. When we tried some police tricks, she relented. She said there were three men, but she knew only one of them. His name was Ashok Singh.

Ashok Singh, she said, was a frequent visitor to the house. She further said she was clueless about where the men may have gone or where they were likely to go. She had relented, but only to a limit. She wouldn't tell us about Surajbhan's house. Even when we slapped her, she didn't provide any more information.

We decided to check out the terrace. It was a congested area and we thought maybe the roofs of the houses were joined, allowing easy movement between houses. The men may have jumped over to another terrace to escape.

When we were running to the terrace, a Sten gun went off by accident. One of our gunners could not control it in the tension. Fortunately, the bullets didn't hit anyone, but there was a loud burst. The boom of the gun wouldn't go unnoticed, we thought, and we became worried about its reaction.

Surajbhan's rival gangs also lived in the vicinity and thinking that it was an attack on them, they could react. We didn't want to open a new front and get engaged in it. We aimed to go after the men who had just escaped.

Nothing happened. There was nothing on the terrace.

We had thought that we would get him that day and close this chapter. We would have avenged the murder of RK Singh.

1

Shriprakash Shukla, *aka Ashok Singh,* whose name spelled terror in Uttar Pradesh in the late 1990s. This is his only photograph available till date.

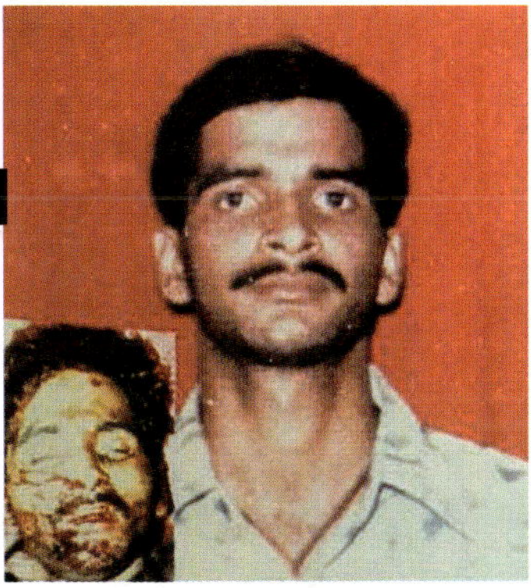

2

Anand Pandey was a close aide of Shriprakash Shukla who died in a police encounter a few days before Shriprakash Shukla's encounter.

3

Surajbhan, a politician from Bihar, who helped Shriprakash Shukla and gave him an AK-47 rifle.

THE STF TEAM

given a grand welcome at the Lucknow airport after the encounter

4 Rajesh Pandey
first from left.

5 Rajesh Pandey
first from right.

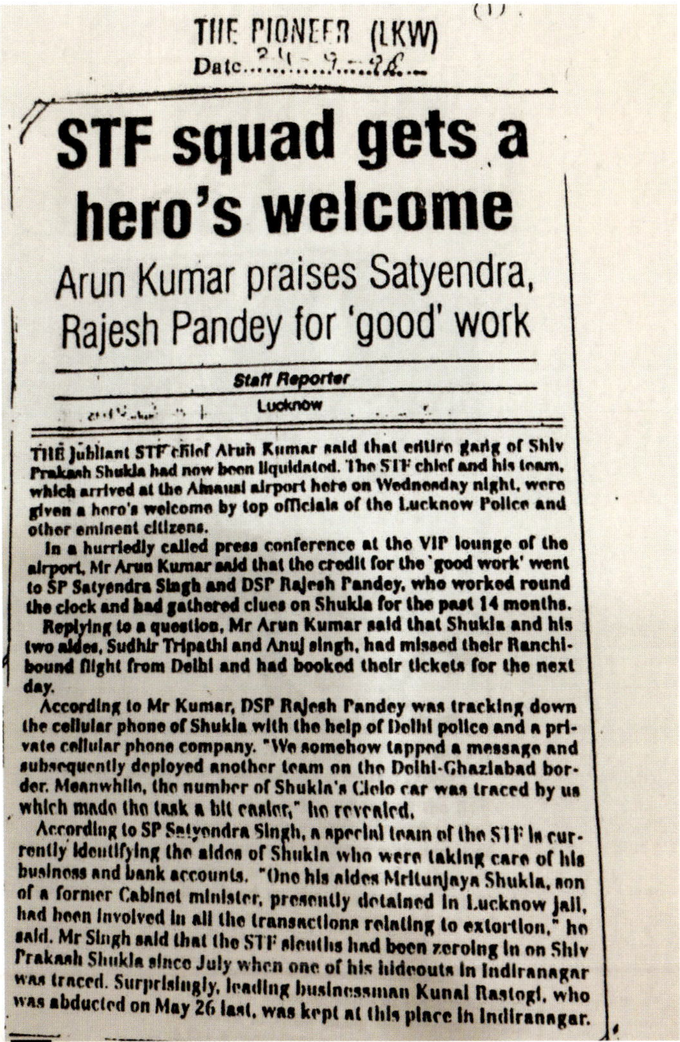

THE PIONEER (LKW)

Date 24-9-98

STF squad gets a hero's welcome

Arun Kumar praises Satyendra, Rajesh Pandey for 'good' work

Staff Reporter

Lucknow

THE jubilant STF chief Arun Kumar said that entire gang of Shiv Prakash Shukla had now been liquidated. The STF chief and his team, which arrived at the Amausi airport here on Wednesday night, were given a hero's welcome by top officials of the Lucknow Police and other eminent citizens.

In a hurriedly called press conference at the VIP lounge of the airport, Mr Arun Kumar said that the credit for the 'good work' went to SP Satyendra Singh and DSP Rajesh Pandey, who worked round the clock and had gathered clues on Shukla for the past 14 months.

Replying to a question, Mr Arun Kumar said that Shukla and his two aides, Sudhir Tripathi and Anuj singh, had missed their Ranchi-bound flight from Delhi and had booked their tickets for the next day.

According to Mr Kumar, DSP Rajesh Pandey was tracking down the cellular phone of Shukla with the help of Delhi police and a private cellular phone company. "We somehow tapped a message and subsequently deployed another team on the Delhi-Ghazlabad border. Meanwhile, the number of Shukla's Cielo car was traced by us which made the task a bit easier," he revealed.

According to SP Satyendra Singh, a special team of the STF is currently identifying the aides of Shukla who were taking care of his business and bank accounts. "One his aides Mritunjaya Shukla, son of a former Cabinet minister, presently detained in Lucknow jail, had been involved in all the transactions relating to extortion," he said. Mr Singh said that the STF sleuths had been zeroing in on Shiv Prakash Shukla since July when one of his hideouts in Indiranagar was traced. Surprisingly, leading businessman Kunal Rastogi, who was abducted on May 26 last, was kept at this place in Indiranagar.

6 Heroes welcomed with tears of happiness as family and police staff surrounded them.

7

Rajesh Pandey with the then Chief Minister, Sh.Kalyan Singh.

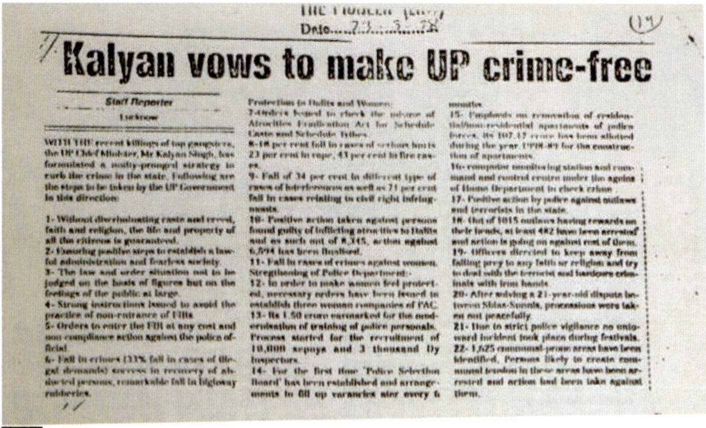

Date.....23.....5.....98

Kalyan vows to make UP crime-free

Staff Reporter

Lucknow

WITH THE recent killings of top gangsters, the UP Chief Minister, Mr Kalyan Singh, has formulated a multy-pronged strategy to curb the crime in the state. Following are the steps to be taken by the UP Government in this direction:

1- Without discriminating caste and creed, faith and religion, the life and property of all the citizens is guaranteed.
2- Ensuring positive steps to establish a lawful administration and fearless society.
3- The law and order situation not to be judged on the basis of figures but on the feelings of the public at large.
4- Strong instructions issued to avoid the practice of non-entrance of FIRs.
5- Orders to enter the FIR at any cost and non compliance action against the police official.
6- Fall in crimes (33% fall in cases of illegal demands) success in recovery of abducted persons, remarkable fall in highway robberies.

Protection to Dalits and Women:
7-Orders issued to check the misuse of Atrocities Eradication Act for Schedule Caste and Schedule Tribes.
8-18 per cent fall in cases of [illegible] hurts, 23 per cent in rape, 43 per cent in fire cases.
9- Fall of 34 per cent in different type of cases of interferences as well as 71 per cent fall in cases relating to civil right infringments.
10- Positive action taken against persons found guilty of inflicting atrocities to Dalits and as such out of 8,345, action against 6,594 has been finalised.
11- Fall in cases of crimes against women.
Stregthening of Police Department:-
12- In order to make women feel protected, necessary orders have been issued to establish three women companies of PAC.
13- Rs 1.50 crore earmarked for the modernisation of training of police personals. Process started for the recruitment of 10,000 sepoys and 3 thousand Dy Inspectors.
14- For the first time 'Police Selection Board' has been established and arrangements to fill up vacancies after every 6 months.
15- Emphasis on renovation of residential/non-residential apartments of police forces. Rs 107.17 crore has been allotted during the year 1998-99 for the construction of apartments.
16- computer monitoring station and command and control centre under the aegies of Home Department to check crime.
17- Positive action by police against outlaws and terrorists in the state.
18- Out of 1015 outlaws having rewards on their heads, at least 482 have been arrested and action is going on against rest of them.
19- Officers directed to keep away from falling prey to any faith or religion and try to deal with the terrorist and hardcore criminals with iron hands.
20- After solving a 21-year-old dispute between Shias-Sunnis, processions were taken out peacefully.
21- Due to strict police vigilance no untoward incident took place during festivals.
22- 1,625 communal-prone areas have been identified. Persons likely to create communal tension in these areas have been arrested and action had been take against them.

8 **Chief Minister Sh Kalyan Singh's** efforts to end the reign of terror led to the creation of the STF.

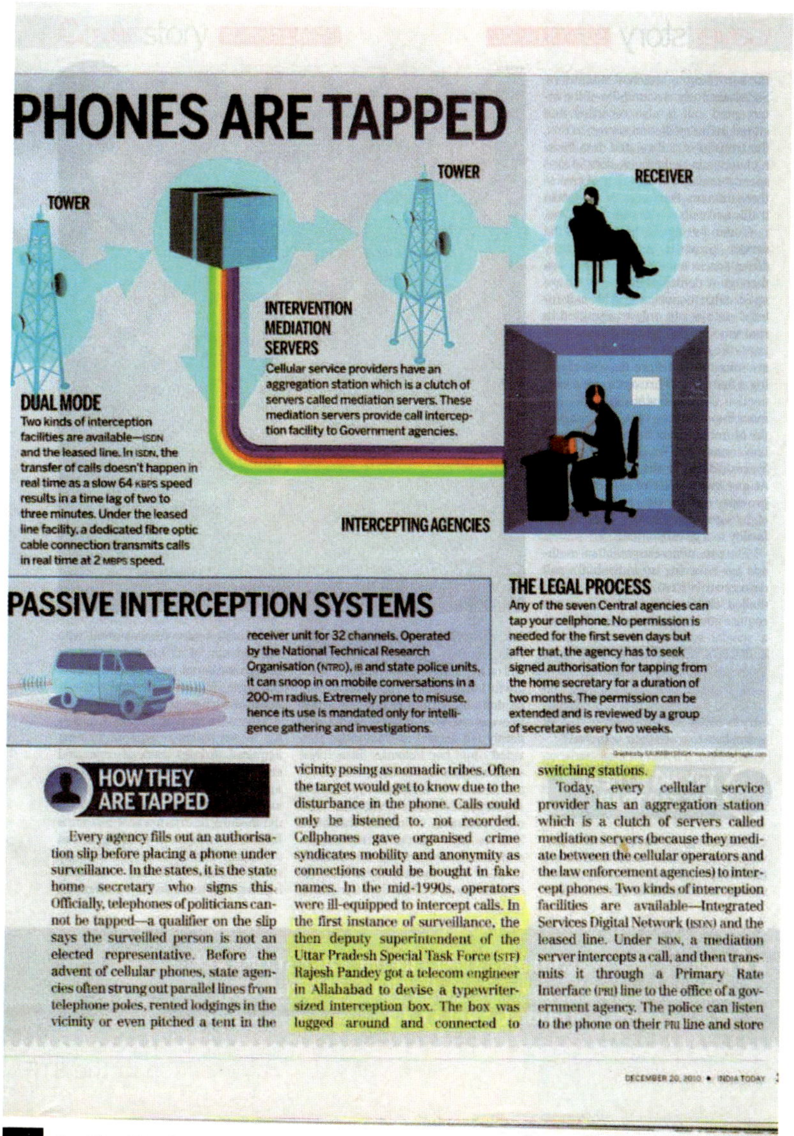

PHONES ARE TAPPED

TOWER

INTERVENTION MEDIATION SERVERS

Cellular service providers have an aggregation station which is a clutch of servers called mediation servers. These mediation servers provide call interception facility to Government agencies.

TOWER

RECEIVER

DUAL MODE

Two kinds of interception facilities are available—ISDN and the leased line. In ISDN, the transfer of calls doesn't happen in real time as a slow 64 KBPS speed results in a time lag of two to three minutes. Under the leased line facility, a dedicated fibre optic cable connection transmits calls in real time at 2 MBPS speed.

INTERCEPTING AGENCIES

PASSIVE INTERCEPTION SYSTEMS

receiver unit for 32 channels. Operated by the National Technical Research Organisation (NTRO), IB and state police units, it can snoop in on mobile conversations in a 200-m radius. Extremely prone to misuse, hence its use is mandated only for intelligence gathering and investigations.

THE LEGAL PROCESS

Any of the seven Central agencies can tap your cellphone. No permission is needed for the first seven days but after that, the agency has to seek signed authorisation for tapping from the home secretary for a duration of two months. The permission can be extended and is reviewed by a group of secretaries every two weeks.

HOW THEY ARE TAPPED

Every agency fills out an authorisation slip before placing a phone under surveillance. In the states, it is the state home secretary who signs this. Officially, telephones of politicians cannot be tapped—a qualifier on the slip says the surveilled person is not an elected representative. Before the advent of cellular phones, state agencies often strung out parallel lines from telephone poles, rented lodgings in the vicinity or even pitched a tent in the vicinity posing as nomadic tribes. Often the target would get to know due to the disturbance in the phone. Calls could only be listened to, not recorded. Cellphones gave organised crime syndicates mobility and anonymity as connections could be bought in fake names. In the mid-1990s, operators were ill-equipped to intercept calls. In the first instance of surveillance, the then deputy superintendent of the Uttar Pradesh Special Task Force (STF) Rajesh Pandey got a telecom engineer in Allahabad to devise a typewriter-sized interception box. The box was lugged around and connected to switching stations.

Today, every cellular service provider has an aggregation station which is a clutch of servers called mediation servers (because they mediate between the cellular operators and the law enforcement agencies) to intercept phones. Two kinds of interception facilities are available—Integrated Services Digital Network (ISDN) and the leased line. Under ISDN, a mediation server intercepts a call, and then transmits it through a Primary Rate Interface (PRI) line to the office of a government agency. The police can listen to the phone on their PRI line and store

DECEMBER 20, 2010 • INDIA TODAY

8 ***India Today* magazine's**
coverage highlighting Rajesh Pandey's contribution in nabbing Shukla.

Various leading dailies
covered the gangster's death,
PRAISING THE EFFORTS OF THE STF

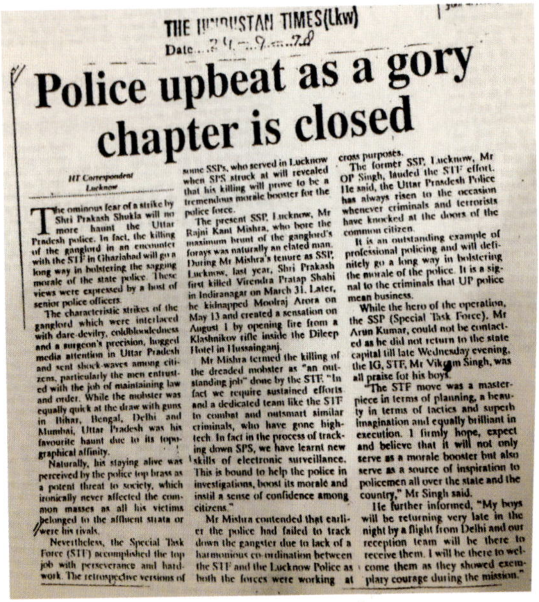

THE HINDUSTAN TIMES (Lkw)
Date... 24-9-98

Police upbeat as a gory chapter is closed

HT Correspondent
Lucknow

The ominous fear of a strike by Shri Prakash Shukla will no more haunt the Uttar Pradesh police. In fact, the killing of the ganglord in an encounter with the STF in Ghaziabad will go a long way in bolstering the sagging morale of the state police. These views were expressed by a host of senior police officers.

The characteristic strikes of the ganglord which were interlaced with dare-devilry, coldbloodedness and a surgeon's precision, hogged media attention in Uttar Pradesh and sent shock-waves among citizens, particularly the men entrusted with the job of maintaining law and order. While the mobster was equally quick at the draw with guns in Bihar, Bengal, Delhi and Mumbai, Uttar Pradesh was his favourite haunt due to its topographical affinity.

Naturally, his staying alive was perceived by the police top brass as a potent threat to society, which ironically never affected the common masses as all his victims belonged to the affluent strata or were his rivals.

Nevertheless, the Special Task Force (STF) accomplished the top job with perseverance and hardwork. The retrospective versions of some SSPs, who served in Lucknow when SPS struck at will revealed that his killing will prove to be a tremendous morale booster for the police force.

The present SSP, Lucknow, Mr Rajni Kant Mishra, who bore the maximum brunt of the ganglord's forays was naturally an elated man. During Mr Mishra's tenure as SSP, Lucknow, last year, Shri Prakash first killed Virendra Pratap Shahi in Indiranagar on March 31. Later, he kidnapped Moolraj Arora on May 13 and created a sensation on August 1 by opening fire from a Klashnikov rifle inside the Dileep Hotel in Hussainganj.

Mr Mishra termed the killing of the dreaded mobster as "an outstanding job" done by the STF. "In fact we require sustained efforts and a dedicated team like the STF to combat and outsmart similar criminals, who have gone high-tech. In fact in the process of tracking down SPS, we have learnt new skills of electronic surveillance. This is bound to help the police in investigations, boost its morale and instil a sense of confidence among citizens."

Mr Mishra contended that earlier the police had failed to track down the gangster due to lack of a harmonious co-ordination between the STF and the Lucknow Police as both the forces were working at cross purposes.

The former SSP, Lucknow, Mr OP Singh, lauded the STF effort. He said, the Uttar Pradesh Police has always risen to the occasion whenever criminals and terrorists have knocked at the doors of the common citizen.

It is an outstanding example of professional policing and will definitely go a long way in bolstering the morale of the police. It is a signal to the criminals that UP police mean business.

While the hero of the operation, the SSP (Special Task Force), Mr Arun Kumar, could not be contacted as he did not return to the state capital till late Wednesday evening, the IG, STF, Mr Vikram Singh, was all praise for his boys.

"The STF move was a masterpiece in terms of planning, a beauty in terms of tactics and superb imagination and equally brilliant in execution. I firmly hope, expect and believe that it will not only serve as a morale booster but also serve as a source of inspiration to policemen all over the state and the country," Mr Singh said.

He further informed, "My boys will be returning very late in the night by a flight from Delhi and our reception team will be there to receive them. I will be there to welcome them as they showed exemplary courage during the mission."

खूंखार हत्यारा श्रीप्रकाश शुक्ल गाजियाबाद में मारा गया

मुठभेड़ में दो अन्य साथी भी मारे गये ■ ए.के. ४७ भी बरामद

श्रीप्रकाश मारा गया

THE PIONEER (LKW)
Date...23...9...98

(32)

Rich rejoice, commoners indifferent to encounter

Pranjan Srivastava

Lucknow

THE thought of 'The Don' aroused terror during his lifetime. In his death, he arouses a strange sense of relief among his potential victims _ the rich traders who shelled out lakhs to escape his AK-47. But, it is sheer indifference among the commonman, who feel his death does not leave their life, which never had any fear from him, any better.

Shiv Prakash Shukla's disappearance from the world of crime has left the reaction sharply divided among the Lucknowites on the lines of elite and common.

As the businessmen's reaction changed from that of disbelief to jubilation on Tuesday evening, Ms Vijay Saxena of Mahanagar summed many in her bafflement: "Will his death bring down the price of onion?"

The trading community were overjoyed as the news of the killing of the UP's most wanted gangster trickled down in the afternoon. The Janpath market had a strange show of traders hugging each other, distributing sweets, as if the festival of Dipawali had come a month earlier.

But, Shukla's terror still reigns their hearts and the apprehension remains. They refused to come on record with their bombastic reactions, fearing what happens if the news proves incorrect.

A leading cloth merchant at Janpath, on the condition of anonymity, said the Janpath traders were jubilant over STF's achievement. "We were the worst suffers of his activities," he said, adding: "However, the real happiness will be if the government ensures that no new Shukla will be born."

Another businessman, owning a restaurant at Hazratganj, said on the request of not disclosing his name, "*Abhi visvas nahi hota hai ki Shri Prakash mara gaya, kahin police ne pachnanne mein galti na kar di ho.* (I cannot believe that Shri Prakash is dead. Hope the police has not faltered in identifying him.)"

For all the joy in the big shops and sprawling showrooms, the commoners said his death will not benefit them in any way. "If crime has to be curbed, the axe should fall on smalltime thieves and chain snatchers who strike on will," said Ms Nutan Pandey, a school teacher and resident of Indira Nagar.

"His death is news for the rich businessman, the politicians and industrialists who were his targets," said Amit Kumar, a resident of Alambagh.

The family members of Kunal Rastogi, who were the latest victim of Shiv Prakash, were not available for reactions.

But away from this difference of opinion among people in general, it was a matter of celebration for the district police. The SSP Mr Rajiv Kant Mishra termed it as the "most outstanding achievement" and congratulated the STF team. Mr S S Baghel, SP (East) said the encounter will not be forgotten for many years and will be a source of inspiration for the cops.

Mr Jitendra Kumar Shahi, SP (Trans-Gomti), when contacted in Delhi, said it had proved that "long arms of law catch up with all, sooner or later". Every criminal should be ready for this gory end before raising his head, he remarked.

THE HINDUSTAN TIMES (Lkw)
Date...23...9...98

Sri Prakash Shukla, two aides shot dead

HT Correspondent

New Delhi

One of the most dreaded gangsters of eastern India, Sri Prakash Shukla, along with his two close associates, were shot dead in an encounter with a combined team of UP police and the Crime Branch of Delhi Police in Vasundhara, Ghaziabad on Tuesday afternoon.

Sri Prakash was carrying a reward of Rs 2 lakh on his head, while his associates had a reward of Rs 20,000 each.

Apart from about 27 sensational abductions and murders, Sri Prakash Shukla was also said to have murdered a Bihar minister and a Uttar Pradesh Member of Legislative Assembly.

Addressing a press conference, Additional Director-General of Police, UP, Mr Ajay Raj Sharma, said that the Special Task Force of UP police and Delhi police had information that Sri Prakash Shukla and his two associates, Anuj Singh and Sudhir Tripathi would be moving towards Delhi from Ghaziabad.

"A trap was laid at Vasundhara, near the Ghaziabad-Delhi border, and soon after the Cielo car (HR-26G-7305) was spotted, there was an exchange of fire between the gangsters and the police team," Mr Sharma said.

A total number of 25 bullets were fired in the encounter from both sides.

The police later recovered two revolvers of 38 bore with 14 live cartridges and Rs 50,000 cash from the car.

According to the police, Sri Prakash's gang had also managed to acquire Klashnikov rifles, dropped in Purulia, from Suraj Bhan, a notorious gangster of Patna.

Last year, Sri Prakash had allegedly killed Upender Vikram Singh, an MLA from Gorakhpur and another minister of Bihar.

Apart from about 27 sensational abductions and murders, Sri Prakash Shukla was also said to have murdered a Bihar minister and a Uttar Pradesh Member of Legislative Assembly

This year, Sri Prakash and his [illegible] owner of a pharmaceutical company from Lucknow. When his father tried to resist his son's abduction, he was shot dead by Sri Prakash. Sri Prakash later released Kunal after taking a ransom of more than Rs one crore.

Sri Prakash had also killed the [illegible] of a Superintendent of Police of Lucknow. The SP, Mr Satyam Vir Singh, was also a part of the team which killed Sri Prakash.

The police said that Sri Prakash was threatening influential people and VIPs for getting contracts and [illegible] in favour of his associates. "It was also alleged that he had been paid a sum of Rs six crore to eliminate Kalyan Singh. However, the information could not be verified," Mr Sharma [illegible] with Suraj Bhan, a notorious gangster of Patna and collected huge amount of arms and ammunition through him.

He is said to have been under the tutelage of a number of politicians and was also allegedly responsible for the murder of Brij Bihari Prasad, who had been given Black Cat commandos for his personal security.

Anuj Singh, who was also killed in the encounter, was the son of a retired sub-inspector of UP police. Both Anuj and Sudhir were the two closest associates of Sri Prakash.

On one occasion, Sri Prakash along with his associates had entered a hotel in Lucknow with Klashnikov rifles and shot dead Vivek Shukla and injured [illegible]

दैनिक जागरण (लखनऊ)
दिनांक 23-9-98

कारगर सिद्ध हुआ स्पेशल टास्क फोर्स का गठन

[illegible]

[illegible]

हिन्दुस्तान (लखनऊ)
दिनांक 23-9-98

कारगर होने लगी है 'स्पेशल टास्क फोर्स'

[illegible]

THE PIONEER (LKW)
Date 23-9-98

STF accomplishes the 'real' job

Staff Reporter
Lucknow

WITHIN A short span, the Special Task Force (STF) sleuths had gunned down about six notorious criminals who were carrying cash rewards on their heads.

However, the real motive behind forming of the STF by the Uttar Pradesh Chief Minister, Mr Kalyan Singh, was achieved when the dreaded gangster Shiv Prakash Shukla was shot dead in a encounter in Ghaziabad on Tuesday forenoon. Two of the accomplices of this killer were also killed.

Soon after its formation, the STF sleuths arrested Sanjeev alias Banni Dwivedi, an active member of Abhay Singh group from Mahanagar area on June 11 last. He later confessed to his involvement in the murder case of Dharmendra Singh, a supporter of the former Lucknow University Students Union general secretary, Anil Singh alias Veeru.

Two weeks later, on June 25, the STF sleuths nabbed one Anand Kumar, who was extorting money in the name of Shiv Prakash Shukla. On July 26, they gunned down Sugreev, a notorious criminal of Barabanki, carrying a reward of Rs 20,000 on his head.

On August 16, The STF team arrested an another hardened criminal, Anil Robert, wanted in a double murder case on August 15. Anil, too, was carrying a reward of Rs 20,000.

A week later, on August 23, the STF personnel gunned down a listed mafia don, Vinod Singh, who was carrying a reward of Rs 50,000 on his head. Vinod was also wanted in over two dozen other crime cases. The sensational encounter took place near the Kukrail forests.

On August 30, the STF sleuths arrested Pikko, a notorious criminal, carrying a reward of Rs 25,000. In yet an another encounter in Varanasi on September 6, the STF team shot dead Pyare Lal Yadav, a close aide of Munna Bajrangi.

The STF adds an another feather in its cap when on September 11 on the Delhi-Karnal border, its sleuths gunned down notorious criminal Yatindar Singh Gujjar. The mafia don, Prem Prakash Singh, alias Munna Bajrangi, carrying a reward of Rs 50,000, was seriously injured in the encounter.

Finally, on Tuesday afternoon, the STF team shot dead the most-ed wanted don of Uttar Pradesh, Shiv Prakash Shukla and two of his aides, Sudhir Tripathi and Anuj Singh, in Ghaziabad.

In frustration, we tossed around the belongings and ransacked the house.

We wanted people to know after we left that UP Police had raided the house. It was important to drive home the point that Mokama was not impregnable.

The car was checked thoroughly. Shriprakash did not even have time to come to the car. He escaped with the weapons, which were probably more important for him, and couldn't bother taking the documents from the glove box of the car.

We found the car's registration papers and two driving licenses.

Meanwhile, the word spread that there had been a police raid. People had also heard the gunshots and there was no reaction probably because the locals found out that it was not by any of the gangs, but by the police. The rooftop sentries had disappeared.

When we were returning from the house, we came across a man on a bicycle coming from the other side.

We stopped him and thinking that he may have seen the men escaping, we asked him, "Did you see people with weapons going this side?"

The man was a local. Mokama has several rival gangs and they always tip off the police about each other to settle scores.

"*Ji sarkar*," he answered without getting off the cycle. "I saw them. One of them had an AK-47; others had pistols."

The man said he had come from across the river for some work in the market. Boats carrying people across the river in Mokama allow cycles and cattle on them.

"I also saw some policemen. I think one of them was an officer. He had a pistol. Three others looked like constables, carrying rifles," the man said, leaving us in awe of his awareness about the police and weapons.

Later, during a discussion with the SP RA in Patna, we learnt that most people in and around Mokama knew about weapons because they brushed with intense gang rivalries on a regular basis.

The bicycle man said he thought the police would nab the men with weapons or there could be firing from both sides so he stopped at a distance to witness the action.

"I saw the man with the AK-47 charge towards the police. The constables ran and the officer dropped his pistol. The three men stopped and giggled at the panic-stricken cops before walking to a boat," the man on the bicycle told us.

Shriprakash escaped on foot and slipped out of our hands. It was immensely demotivating for us, especially after having come so close to getting him.

Soon, we saw the ASP and the three constables walking towards us.

"You let him go," Satyendra Vir lashed out in anger.

The officer didn't say anything.

"You have a Glock pistol. We in UP Police haven't ever seen such a sophisticated weapon, and yet you allowed them to go," Satyendra Vir continued to shout at them.

The Glock pistols, named after its manufacturer Gaston Glock, are self-loading, semi-automatic handguns with a polymer frame. The firearm, which was first inducted into the Austrian military and debuted in the Indian police in 1995, is lightweight and does not go off accidentally. The new modern duty pistol had not been inducted into the UP Police until then, but officers of Bihar Police had been provided the handguns.

"You could have at least fired in the air. We would have heard the gunshot and got the cue. We came with such a big force, had so many weapons. There was no way he could have gone out of our hands today."

"The constables deserted me," the officer replied timidly.

He was a young officer. A direct IPS. It's been twenty-two years since that day and he must have become an ADG or at least an IG somewhere. It would be imprudent to name him. It must have been a very bitter experience for him that day.

We came back to Murali Lal Meena and told him that we had failed in our operation. Satyendra Vir curtly said, "Ask the ASP why."

When Meena heard what had happened, he also got very angry. He lambasted his men. "You have brought shame to the Bihar Police." He said the officer could have run aside and fired in the air. "There was so much force with you. You shouldn't have come without him today," he said.

The officer remained shy and nervous.

Shriprakash had cleared out of our reach and there was no use crying over spilled milk now.

We requested Meena sir to make arrangements for taking the Ambassador to Lucknow. We told him that this car and the documents found in it would help us take our investigation forward.

One driver and two constables were deputed to drive the Ambassador to Lucknow. One person from our team also travelled in the car.

We went to Patna Railway Station with a heavy heart. The state plane had returned to Lucknow the previous evening after dropping us.

We reached Lucknow the next morning and had to start working on the documents after briefing the SSP about our failed operation in Mokama. We had found RK Singh's missing pistol. That was evidence that our officer was killed by Shriprakash.

The driving license found in the car was in the name of Dhirendra Singh and bore the address of Sultanpur. The local police were sent to every address recovered from the documents found in the Ambassador. Dhirendra Singh's family said he had not visited them for over six months. He had been with some criminals from Gorakhpur, they said. The police got information that Dhirendra Singh was staying in Faizabad.

In Faizabad, gun dealer Paramjit Singh Balli had the dubious record of supplying firearms and cartridges to criminals. People from far and wide visited his shop in Rakabganj to procure cartridges for their illegal weapons. Balli sold ammunition for all bores and was quite popular amongst a lot of gangs. We were sure he would lead us to Dhirendra Singh.

When the police went to him to inquire about Dhirendra Singh, he proved to be more forthcoming than we had expected.

"Dhirendra Singh was here about two hours ago," Balli told the police. "He was heavily drunk." Balli knew where Dhirendra Singh lived. He was put in a police jeep and asked to take the cops to where Dhirendra Singh was putting up.

The police found Dhirendra Singh fast asleep in the house. When the cops tried to shake him out of slumber, he woke up with a start.

Dhirendra Singh was brought to Lucknow. During the interrogation process, he told us about a house in the posh locality of Gomti Nagar that Shriprakash had rented. One team took him along with them to that house.

It was in Viram Khand. It had big bungalows full of officers and affluent families. Shriprakash lived on the ground floor of one such bungalow. His part of the bungalow was locked. We broke the lock and went inside. A Gypsy with a red light was parked there. The household items there suggested that at least three people had been staying there.

The house belonged to a very senior IAS officer. He was questioned about his tenant. He said he had let it out through a broker, who had told him that Shriprakash was the chairman of some multinational company and would visit Lucknow occasionally for work. The broker also told the house owner that there was a woman with them because the landlord insisted on giving his house only to a family. They had two vehicles - an Ambassador and a Gypsy - both with red lights.

We asked Dhirendra Singh about the woman. She was Manju Singh from Barra in Kanpur. She often visited Shriprakash in Lucknow. Dhirendra Singh led us to her.

She was interrogated. She said she got money for staying with him occasionally. Whenever she came to Lucknow, she said Shriprakash would take her shopping. He splurged on her and even gave her money. After a few days, he would drop her off in Kanpur, telling her that the group was going out for work.

She said she didn't know his real name. She was a woman, so we didn't put her through strict interrogation and allowed her to go. But she remained under our radar. Her phone was also put on surveillance.

Dhirendra Singh proved to be an important catch. He spilled the beans on the gang's activities seven days ago. Dhirendra Singh hadn't met the gang in the past week.

He told us about all the crimes that the gang had committed, the people who were with Shriprakash on those operations, people who sheltered him, who supplied weapons to him and from where he got the cartridges. Dhirendra Singh was a storehouse of information.

After sustained interrogation for many days, we found complete details about Shriprakash and his gang for the first time. We got hold of descriptions of every member of the gang.

Anand Pandey was an introvert, but quite daring. Sudhir Tripathi was a smooth talker and Shriprakash's flunkey. They were permanent fixtures in the gang. Anuj Pratap Singh and Rajan Tiwari were floating members. Rajan Tiwari was originally from Gorakhpur, but his area of operation was Patna and nearby areas. Anuj Pratap Singh was the son of a police officer. He had worked with an airline and spoke fluent English.

We found that Shriprakash never took more than four people to a crime. In some cases, Surajbhan sent some local men to tag along with them, but generally the rule was not to have more than four people. He said the smaller the team, the greater the security of the gang. His logic was – if there were more people during crimes, there were chances of one of them getting caught or getting lured by the rival gang. This, he would say, would be disastrous and may even prove to be fatal for the gang.

Anand Pandey, Sudhir Tripathi, Shriprakash Shukla and Rajan Tiwari constituted the core group. Anuj Pratap Singh and Satyavrat Rai were the new entries. In most operations, there were only Anand Pandey, Sudhir Tripathi and Shriprakash Shukla. In Bihar operations, they would keep Rajan Tiwari and Satyavrat Rai with them. Anuj Pratap Singh was also present in some operations in Bihar, but he was a considerably new hanger-on.

The gang's adda in Lucknow was Pawan Pandey's office near Shubham Cinema on Cantonment Road. Pandey, who was an MLA from Akbarpur in Ambedkar Nagar district, enjoyed the newfound glory, thanks to Shriprakash. He found it easy to get government contracts after Shriprakash killed Satyendra Singh alias Satyendra Langda, a mafia who pocketed all PWD and irrigation departments' tenders. The man was killed on the Lucknow–Faizabad Road in February 1996 at the insistence of Pawan Pandey.

But being the debauched man that Shriprakash was, he got involved with Pawan Pandey's wife and would stay in his house when in Faizabad. Pawan Pandey "fled" to Bombay when he found out that he was a cuckold.

After escaping from Mokama, Shriprakash and his gang fled to Kathmandu. For the first time, they were scared of the police. We had gotten so close and were on the verge of arresting them. The police went with a big force to raid the house and had precise information. Shriprakash suspected that someone from the gang was a mole and was secretly passing information to the police.

This is a tendency of criminal gangs – when the police get precise information about their movements or hideouts, they doubt their own men.

He told his associates that they needed to be circumspect and guarded; otherwise they may soon come face to face with the police.

The gang ran to Pappu Dev in Viratnagar. Pappu Dev arranged for the group to stay at a hotel owned by a police officer. Pappu Dev informed them that there was no danger from the police. "The Nepal police won't bother you and the police from UP or Bihar cannot even enter this place," he told them, adding that they needed to, however, be careful of Dev's rival gangs.

Shriprakash's gang was flush with money. They had just extorted big ransom money from two kidnappings. Every three or four days, they would drive to Kathmandu for gallivanting around and revelry.

One day, during a drinking party, Sudhir Tripathi, Anand Pandey, Rajan Tiwari and Pappu Dev got sloshed, but Shriprakash didn't even touch alcohol. When the party got over and someone wanted to drive, Shriprakash forbade them. He said they were all drunk, and he would take the wheel.

They came to the hotel and were having food when Shriprakash began a spiel about the ill-effects of alcohol on a gang – "Our war for dominance isn't over. Shahi's men are at our heels. People often look for weaknesses in a gang to break it. If people find out that the gang members are fond of drinking, they will use this to get you drunk and try to get information out of you. Then all of us will be killed. You should give up drinking; it's not good for our gang's survival."

Pappu Dev was a local ganglord. He didn't like Shriprakash's harangue. Rajan Tiwari also felt the sermon was misplaced. But no one said anything and retired to sleep.

When they woke up the next morning, Shriprakash was missing. People looked for him. Anand Pandey said he must have gone lusting after some woman. "He was giving us *gyan* last evening and see what he is up to. But don't worry; he will be back soon. He must have gotten drunk with the woman and will be here when he sobers up," Anand said reassuringly.

Soon Shriprakash walked in. As if Pappu Dev was itching to get back to him. "*Aa gaye*? Don't you know that all big criminals get killed because of women? This habit of yours, and not alcohol, will get us killed someday," he mocked Shriprakash. "Use of women is the easiest tool to intrude into a gang. Hope you know that."

Shriprakash didn't say anything and sauntered into the dining area for breakfast.

Later in the day, they were discussing how they needed to lay hands on a big catch. They said among themselves that if they got someone who could plunk down big money, around one or two crores, they could relax for some time. The gang had made money through ransom and understood that this was the easiest and fastest route to prosperity. They said the police were hot on his trail, and committing a big murder would be skating on thin ice; kidnapping would be a safer bet.

Shriprakash got up and said, "Let me go and speak to my men in Lucknow. I will ask them to provide the kundali of someone really wealthy. They need to be activated." As he was walking out, he informed that he needed to speak to his family to ask about their health too.

Over the next few days, it became his routine. Every day, around noon, he would slip out after lunch. He would say that he went out to walk the streets.

One day, Anand Pandey asked him about a safe PCO from where he could call his family. "I haven't spoken to them in a long time," he said.

Shriprakash told him to go to the fruit market. "There are two entries. Go to the rear one; you will find four PCOs there in a row," he told Anand. "They are located in a congested area; no one comes there and there's no danger of the police either."

Anand drove to the fruit market, but even after searching for the row of PCOs, he couldn't find it. He stopped at a fruit seller. After buying some apples and bananas, he asked for the PCOs.

The seller said, "Why do you need four PCOs in a row? There's one there that you may use." Anand Pandey went into the PCO. It seemed like a safe place. A young Nepali boy was sitting at the counter. Anand told him that he wanted to make a call to India, but the boy didn't understand Hindi very well, so he pushed a piece of paper towards him to scribble the number.

Anand wrote down the number and went inside a small cubicle where a telephone was kept. The numbers had to be dialled from the phone outside the cabin. The operator would signal the person inside to pick up the receiver when the line would go through.

Before dialling, the boy looked at the number on the paper. It looked familiar. He opened the register and found it entered a day before. He called Anand and showed it to him.

Anand thought maybe the police were trying to call his home. The bills were also stapled in the register. He looked at the bill from the previous day. It read 450 rupees. This was a huge amount in those days. The call duration was a little more than forty-five minutes.

ISD rate for international calls was higher and even though Gorakhpur was barely fifty kilometres away, it was expensive to call a number there. Anand wondered who may have called his home and spoken for so long. He told the boy to dial another number. Anand called some Pawan Pandey. He was not at home. Anand told the receiver to tell Pawan that Bhaiyya called from Nepal.

After finishing this call, he pored over the register. His home number had been called several times. Someone was calling his home every day, between noon and 1 p.m. and talking for long.

When Anand returned to the hotel, Shriprakash asked him if he was successful at locating the PCOs.

"Yes bhaiyya, I found those PCOs. They were safe to make calls."

"Is everyone okay at home?" Shriprakash asked.

"Yes," Anand replied.

Shriprakash heaved a sigh of relief. Anand hadn't found out, he thought.

Chapter 9
The Split

That night, Anand Pandey couldn't sleep a wink. Something was troubling him deeply. He had an inkling about what might be happening every afternoon, but did not react.

The next day, Shriprakash got on with his usual routine. Nothing had changed for him. He jumped into the car and left the hotel around noon. When he was gone, Anand told Sudhir and Rajan that he had a stomach ache.

"Let me go and get a Balargan tablet," he said.

He hired a taxi from outside the hotel and told the driver to take him to the fruit market. When the taxi was nearing the destination, he stopped it and got down about 100 metres away from the PCO.

He spotted the car that they had used to travel to Viratnagar outside Siddharth Hotel.

So Shriprakash was at the PCO, Anand thought.

Anand could have confronted him, but decided against it and instead walked to a nearby tea shop from where he could monitor activities in the PCO. It was 12.30 p.m. Shriprakash scampered out around 1 p.m. and left in the car.

Anand was seething with anger. He went to the PCO. The young boy from the previous day was not there. He told the man sitting at the counter that he had come the previous day too.

"I forgot to carry my diary. Can you please help me with the number from the register?" he asked the PCO man.

The operator pushed the register towards Anand. The last

entry was his home number. The bill was 350 rupees. That meant that the call lasted for around forty minutes.

His blood was pumping heavily through his veins. But he controlled himself. "I think the boy here yesterday forgot to record the number in the register. Let me come back with the diary," he said and dashed out. He went to another PCO that he had spotted near the place where Shriprakash had parked.

He dialed the number. The phone was answered swiftly after only one ring. Anand's sister answered. Before he could say anything, she blurted, "Haven't you left? You said you were going to the hotel."

"*Main Munna bol raha hoon* (I am Munna)," Anand said, as he frothed at the mouth. The sister felt discomposed. She disconnected the line.

The mystery was solved.

Anand returned to the hotel. Sudhir asked him what took him so long. "The medical shop is right here."

Anand said he wanted to take a stroll to get relief from the ache. "I went to the market and had a cup of tea. I wanted Balargan to start working before I walked back," he said as he stared at Shriprakash. His eyes were burning embers.

Shriprakash had a silver-coloured digital diary; he was looking into it.

A little later, Shriprakash suggested to the group that they should be moving now.

"We have idled here long enough. Now we should get back to work. There's a tender waiting for us in Lucknow. Let's go and get it," he said.

No one said anything. They packed their bags and put them in the car. Pappu Dev was informed about the departure, and the gang left.

When they were approaching Patna – must have been about fifty kilometres away – Anand bent towards Shriprakash, who was at the driver's seat, and said, "Bhai, please drop Rajan Tiwari and me to the Patna office of Surajbhan dada. We need to be there for some work."

"What work?" Shriprakash asked, his eyes fixed on the road ahead.

Anand said his niece's wedding was scheduled for two months later, but he hadn't had time to shop for her. "It is not wise to go shopping in Gorakhpur or Lucknow. Rajan Tiwari knows people here; he will take me shopping," he said from the back seat and gently pressed Rajan Tiwari's hand.

He got the cue. "Yes bhaiyya. It's his niece's wedding and his family needs to give a lot of items. Patna is good for shopping. We shall be here for a few days and then join you in Lucknow," he echoed Anand.

Shriprakash said, "Okay. I was also thinking of calling dada."

They reached Surajbhan's office in Kankadbagh, parked the car outside. Anand and Shriprakash went inside, while others waited outside.

After the pleasantries, Anand burst out, "Dada, I cannot work with him anymore."

It put the cat among the pigeons. Surajbhan was taken aback.

"What's the matter?" he asked. He had never imagined Anand and Shriprakash as two entities. For Surajbhan, they were one.

Anand told Surajbhan everything. He said he could never think that Shriprakash could be so treacherous. "I feel ashamed of even telling you what he's been up to for the past few days," Anand said in frustration.

"Is this correct, Ashok Singh?" Surajbhan asked.

"Could it be only my fault, dada?"

Anand stood up in rage. "Dada, ask him to shut up! If he utters one more word, I will either kill him or get killed."

Surajbhan calmed him down. He said that both of them were his gems. "Virendra Shahi wouldn't have been killed if it weren't for you two. We avenged Chhutkun Shukla with your help. I would have been happy if you stayed together but when things get murky, it is best to part ways. Otherwise, the entire gang suffers," Surajbhan spoke like a wise, elderly man.

Anand requested Surajbhan to get him his weapons. Surajbhan said, "Fair enough, Ashok Singh give him the weapons. Give him one .45mm pistol, two .9mm pistols and a hundred cartridges."

He told Dhirendra and Rajan Tiwari to get the firearms.

"Ashok Singh, you may leave now."

When Shriprakash got up to leave, Surajbhan told him, "You waste a lot of time and money on women. History is full of stories about people in the underworld who met their end because of women. You should keep your mission in mind. If you are so fond of sex, go to whores. There's no dearth of red-light districts. Spend money, but not time. What you have done is unpardonable; betraying on your men is a sin."

Previously too, Shriprakash lusted after young women outside kindergartens in Lucknow and Janpath. Manju Singh was his companion when he went looking for rented accommodations.

She would pose as his wife. Shriprakash would shower her with gifts and take her shopping. We later found out that he also called prostitutes to his Delhi flat. As a matter of fact, he missed a flight to Ranchi because he had summoned a Russian call girl the night before and overslept after a wild night of sex and booze. But there was one woman he was emotionally attached to. He was in love with the daughter of a government engineer. We later found out from the call recordings that he spoke to her about love and longing.

Surajbhan asked Shriprakash to decide whether he wanted to take his advice or not. Shriprakash meekly said, "Of course, yes."

"Then you shouldn't get into his path now. I don't want to hear that you both have meddled with each other," Surajbhan advised.

Dhirendra and Rajan had brought the weapons.

Shriprakash paid him respects and left. Sudhir and Dhirendra were with him on the journey to Lucknow.

Surajbhan said he would get Anand, Rajan and Satyavrat dropped at Gorakhpur. "Lie low for some time. Go to your relatives. If there's a problem, let me know, I will organize everything."

They left in Surajbhan's car. When they were out of Mokama, Satyavrat asked Anand Pandey, "Bhai, what happened?"

Anand broke down. "I knew that he was a philanderer, but I continued with him because of my dreams. But he is a filthy man, really filthy," he said amid sobs.

Anand recalled how Niraj Singh killed Hriday Chand and Shriprakash killed Dubey. "You know what? Both Hriday Chand

and Dubey were his friends. But we continued together because I wanted to make it big and it was not possible alone. But look at his depravity!"

Rajan Tiwari and Satyavrat were quietly listening to Anand. "In all the incidents that dada often mentions, what did he actually do? I was the one who emptied bullets into people's heads every single time," Anand said, now sobering down.

There was silence in the car for some time. "I need a car," Anand said looking towards Satyavrat.

"Don't worry. MLA Devendra of Bihar has sent me an Esteem which is parked in Vipin's house in Mohaddipur. I will tell him to bring it to Gol Ghar. You can have it from there," Satyavrat said.

When they were close to Gorakhpur, he called Vipin to bring the car to Gol Ghar. "Clean it and fill up the fuel tank," he told him.

In Gorakhpur, Satyavrat got off Surajbhan's car and left for Lucknow. Rajan Tiwari and Anand Pandey also started for Lucknow in the Esteem after seeing off Surajbhan's men who came to see them. They drove straight to Satyavrat's Indira Nagar house in Lucknow.

Anand and Satyavrat chatted throughout the night. They were sceptical about Shriprakash's promise to dada – about not crossing their paths. "You cannot take him at face value. He is eccentric," they both agreed. They feared that Shriprakash might kill them.

"He is greedy. He can bump off anyone for money. Didn't you see how he killed Gandhi and his gang in their sleep?" Anand wondered.

Satyavrat changed the topic. He said they had to chalk out their next moves. "Let me put you through to MLA Devendra tomorrow. He has been asking me to do something for him for a long time. He has sent the Esteem as an advance for the work. He has promised to give me an AK-47 and some other weapons if we could accomplish the work for him."

Anand got excited when he heard about the offer. "An AK-47 is precisely what we need. We have worked with AK-47 all this while and without that, we may be handicapped," he said.

The next day, they spoke to the Bihar MLA from a PCO. MLA Devendra told them to come to Patna right away. "Please come and finish it for me. I am very perturbed and this needs to be done urgently," he pleaded with Anand. The MLA said he would organise everything for them in Patna.

They returned to Satyavrat's house and slept the whole day. At night, Babloo Tiwari, Rajan Tiwari and Anand Pandey started for Patna in the Esteem. They were desperate to show Shriprakash down.

Anand was not pompous. He preferred to stay quiet, but he was a hardened criminal and an immaculate shooter. He let Shriprakash do the talking. Even when he sometimes answered phone calls, he would pass them on to Shriprakash. His mantra in life was – eat, sleep and focus on work. Anand cared a lot for his family, especially his sister.

When they reached Banaras, Anand said he had an unfinished assignment here. Hriday Chand had given money to one Sengar for getting him a job in the railway. He got some more people to pay Sengar for the job. But it was a fraud – they never got the job and the money was lost. Sengar had become associated with a liquor contractor and refused to return the money to Hriday Chand and others. He would even threaten them. Hriday Chand was broke and needed the money, but Sengar didn't return the amount.

Meanwhile, Niraj Singh killed Hriday Chand.

Anand said he wanted to recover the money from Sengar and give it to Hriday Chand's family. "This maybe of a great help for them," he said.

Rajan Tiwari didn't approve of this as they were headed for a bigger operation. "We can settle this on our return from Patna," he reasoned, but this was more important for Anand. "This may be a good omen for us," he said.

They knocked at Sengar's door around seven in the morning. He came out and recognized Anand immediately.

"How did you come, bhaiyya?" he asked with bewilderment.

Anand told him that he had come to recover Hriday Chand's money. "You thought you could swindle it out of Hriday Chand because he is no more," Anand said barging into the house.

Sengar's wife and his three children were also there. Anand said he didn't have much time. "Give me the money," he thundered.

Sengar said he didn't have a penny that day. He said he needed time to arrange the amount.

Anand pulled out a pistol. He said, "I will put it back only after you give me the money or I will shoot you in the head."

The wife and the kids recoiled in horror. The youngest kid, who must have been around two, began to cry. Sengar said he could do whatever he wanted, but the fact was that there was no money with him in the house that day. He also tried to lull his child into believing that his uncle was using a toy gun.

Anand pumped all the bullets in the magazine into Sengar's head, got up and bolted the door from outside before leaving for Patna.

They were in Patna the next morning. The MLA had asked them to call and inform him upon entering the city. He said they would find a man in a white kurta-pajama a little ahead of the income tax office. "He will take you to the flat where you are going to stay."

As the Esteem reached the income tax office, Anand spotted a Zen parked there. Three men were sitting in the car. On seeing the Esteem, one of them got out. He was wearing a white kurta-pajama. He asked Anand his name. Upon confirming his identity, he asked them to follow him to the flat. It was on the first floor. It only had a caretaker who doubled as a cook. Anand asked him about the MLA.

The caretaker said that the MLA would come around 11 a.m. In the meantime, they could take a bath and get ready. "Tell me what you want to eat. I will have it ready for you," he said.

They had showers and ate breakfast. The MLA came at 11.30 a.m. Without beating around the bush, he came straight to the point. He told them about the man to be killed. "I have brought five lakh rupees for the operation. An AK-47 and other weapons are in my car."

Anand Pandey was delighted from within.

The MLA continued, "Keep all the weapons and take the money, but please complete the work for me," he said.

"I don't take advance payment for contracts," Anand announced proudly.

The MLA failed to notice Anand's attempt to fish for

compliments. The MLA continued in an urgent voice, "It is up to you whether you take the money now or after completing the assignment. I am letting you know that the amount is already arranged."

Anand told him the requirement. "We need a local man to help us draw up the kundali of the target, and it may take a couple of days to spill his blood."

"Kundali?" the MLA asked incredulously.

"Yes, kundali. One kundali is prepared by astrologers that has details of birth, death, life, profession, family, children, etc. We draw up people's *maran* kundali," Anand said. He explained to the MLA how their kundali included the possible place of murder, the exit plan, the number of people on the operation, the number of Rahus and Ketus who accompany the target, the weapons that they have, etc. They also needed to figure out how they could escape the police.

The MLA smiled. He said he would get them a local man in an hour.

"Not today," Anand said. "Today we want to rest. Send him tomorrow morning at around 7 a.m."

The MLA agreed. "My man will help you identify the target, but he won't be with you during the operation. I don't want to risk the life of my man. And if he is caught, my name will come out. My name will come up anyway, but I will work my way around it. But if my man is caught, it will be my end. Just make sure that you inform me within ten minutes of finishing the work," he said.

After the MLA left, Anand and others went out and roamed the local market for some time. That day, they went to bed early.

The man was there the next morning. They all left around eight. The MLA had told them to use his car even for recce. The Esteem was parked in his garage.

They reconnoitered the area the whole day. The target was identified, the routes were noted and the calculations were done.

They took three days to plan the operation. When they called the MLA to tell him that they were ready, he repeated his request, "Please inform me as soon as you can after killing the man. Say within five to ten minutes."

The next day, they went to a railway crossing where they had planned to shoot the target. The MLA had given them an Ambassador car. It was parked on the roadside. When they spotted the car of the target, Anand got down with his .45mm pistol. As the man in the car approached the Ambassador, Anand pulled the trigger and blew his brains out.

The driver jumped out of the running car, which swerved sharply and hit a pole. Rajan and Babloo shot the other people in the car. They found one AK-47, two country-made pistols, one revolver and three .315 bore rifles in the car.

They got back into the Ambassador and decamped with the weapons. As promised, he let the MLA know that the work was completed. After travelling for about ten kilometres, they found a narrower bylane on the left. The Ambassador took that road. After some time, Anand told Rajan to throw away the rifles from the running car at an interval of two kilometres.

When Babloo asked why he wanted to get rid of rifles, Anand smiled like a pro and said, "You guys are greenhorns."

He then explained to them. "When the police will arrive at the crime spot, they will first collect the empty cartridges. It will take them about half an hour. Then some villagers will inform them that a rifle is found on the roadside. Soon other rifles will also be found. By that time, there would be senior officers also on the scene. They will order the men to surround the villages, thinking that we will be there. The houses will be searched. This exercise will take them a few hours and by that time, we will be out of their reach."

Anand lectured them that they needed to know the workings of the police to be successful criminals.

In the evening, the MLA met them at the agreed-upon place. He brought with him six lakh rupees. "Although I promised to pay five, but because I am very happy that the work has been smoothly completed in such a short time, I would like you to take six," he said. An AK-47, two pistols and a revolver were also given.

The MLA told them to leave as soon as possible. "Don't worry about me – I will manage," he said.

They requested the MLA to drop them outside the Bihar border and asked him to have someone take their Esteem there. Once out of the state, they would get into their car, they told him.

Soon, the Esteem was speeding towards Lucknow.

Chapter 10
Anand Pandey Is Dead

The next morning, at around 5 a.m., they reached Satyavrat Rai's house in Indira Nagar. They got off near Lekhraj Market, and Satyavrat was asked to take the car to a local garage and keep it there.

They were tired and slept the whole day. In the evening, Bhuwar Rai, Satyavrat Rai's relative in Marutipuram, came to Indira Nagar. When they sat down to talk, Anand said he wanted to buy a Zen and shift his family out of Gorakhpur.

"We need big money for this," he said.

Rajan Tiwari said the family was living comfortably in Gorakhpur and he felt there was no need to move them.

"He is a filthy man and can harm my family," Anand couldn't get Shriprakash off his mind. "What he's done is still pinching me like a sore wound. He is greedy and immoral. He infiltrated my family. I will look for a good place in Delhi or Ghaziabad and will move them there."

Anand told Bhuwar to scout for him. "Look for a tender that can pay us one or two crores," he said sounding desperate for money. But he was desperate for much more – to prove to Shriprakash that he could operate without him.

Bhuwar was an old hand. He could see Anand's anguish.

"We did all the hard work and he made a name for himself. The businessmen and traders panic upon hearing his name and pay him. Let us make money from this tender and then I will show him his place," Anand said, clearly sounding grumpy.

The gang said they had committed a killing only a day before and that they should cool off for a few days, but Anand didn't have time to relax. "*Shanti se baithe to wo maar dega* (If we lie low, he will kill us)," he mumbled.

The four of them hailed a three-wheeler and went to Bhuwar's house, where he had organised good, non-vegetarian food for everyone. Before returning to Indira Nagar, Anand said pointing at this watch, "10 a.m. tomorrow."

When they assembled at the Indira Nagar house the next morning, Satyavrat reminded everyone that Shriprakash had gotten him to make a kundali of the owner of Lekhraj Dollar and Vivek Ladhani, who owned a bottling plant.

Vivek Ladhani's kidnapping has already been mentioned. The distressed police had an egg on their faces when a second big businessman was abducted. People said, "*Phir utha le gaya aur police kuch nahi kar payee* (They have kidnapped a man again and the police couldn't do anything)."

They said the government had formed a special unit with possibly the best minds to work on crime, but they too seemed helpless before Shriprakash who remained unabated and struck with impunity. Our efforts had resulted in naught and it was frustrating to look inefficient.

The family paid a big ransom and Ladhani returned home after a week.

All along, the police had believed that Shriprakash was behind Ladhani's kidnapping. It was only later that we found out that wasn't the case.

In the Indira Nagar house, Satyavrat and Bhuwar were told to find out the location of the tenders that day. They first went to Lekhraj Dollar, but the employees told them that the owner had gone to Delhi and won't be back before a week.

Ladhani was next. They got him, extorted money and released him.

The SSP wanted us to put Ladhani through sustained questioning to get clues about where the gang may have kept them. Ladhani told us things in bits and pieces. When we put everything together, we concluded that the businessman was held captive in a flat in Delhi.

The SSP told all of us to go to Delhi. "There's no use being here. Go there and look for Delhi numbers in the CDR of Ladhani's mobile phone. I am hopeful we would stumble upon something there," he said.

The informers had been taking us for a ride. Whenever information came, we rushed to the place. Then came another piece of information. Another place. We went there too, but it turned out to be futile.

One day, we got a tip-off that a man matching the profile of Shriprakash was travelling in an air-conditioned train coach. The informant gave us the berth number. This was a vital piece of information and we couldn't ignore it.

We rushed to the Lucknow Railway Station. The Government Railway Police (GRP) and Railway Protection Force (RPF) were against uniformed men swamping a reserved coach. We remained in plainclothes most of the time, but the district police had also been called, and they were in uniform. The GRP and RPF said there would be chaos in the coach, so everyone was told to be in civil attire.

I remember Vijay Bhushan was the SP RA. He was also there. He told a constable to take off his t-shirt, flinging his police shirt at him. There was no problem with the khaki pants.

The train came. We went in and found a man on the berth. He was covered by a white sheet. Our men dragged him from his feet and before he could react, he was carried outside.

"*Mil gaya, mil gaya.*"

Crowds gathered on the platform. It was decided to take the man out of the premises for his own safety. Some constables brought the luggage behind us.

When he hit the ground, punches began raining on him and he was kicked in all possible places. The man kept pleading, saying he was neither Shriprakash nor knew anyone by that name. His daughter, who must also have been travelling with him, had also followed the police. She was howling and saying that her father's name was Lallan Singh and they were from Begusarai in Bihar.

But the police had "found" Shriprakash and wouldn't listen to anything.

We realized the blunder only when the policemen who had seen Shriprakash in real life were called for identification and they said this man wasn't him. But before this, we had upended his suitcases, rummaged through his wallet, diary, and checked his pockets several times. It turned out that he was taking his daughter home from Banasthali Vidyapeeth for the holidays.

The train had left. We apologised to him profusely. He was in a daze. We took them to a police station and arranged a vehicle to take them to Begusarai.

We found a photo album in his luggage. It had photos of weddings, family functions and religious events. We kept it in the hope that we may find photos of Shriprakash or his gang members in it – it is unlikely for the informer to have been completely off the mark.

The purpose of mentioning this incident is to tell you that people also settled personal scores in the name of providing information about the gang. So many people were harassed because someone told us about their links with Shriprakash. Some of these men were even kept in custody for a few days and when we found out that the information was incorrect, we would sheepishly apologise to them.

The team finally arrived in Delhi. We got in touch with PP Singh, an inspector in one of the Delhi police stations. He was a relative of Tevatiya. Delhi Police, especially the crime branch, had a better idea about the workings of mobile phones and CDRs. Mobile phones came there earlier than they were introduced in Lucknow.

We told Singh that we had the CDR of Ladhani's father, and we were trying to find out the place of captivity.

PP Singh turned out to be a great help. All the PCOs were located. We went from one PCO to the other, and finally to the one where we found clues. The PCO operator told us that the men who made those calls came from a flat in Dilshad Garden.

We checked the flat. It was locked. Neighbours told us that some people visit the flat occasionally.

PP Singh arranged for a man to keep a watch on the flat. "Tell us when you spot someone here," he was told.

Meanwhile, Anand Pandey had shifted his family to Delhi. He had bought a Zen, his favourite car. He said no UP Police or Bihar Police vehicle could match the car for speed. Their rumbustious jeeps could not chase it. After parting with Shriprakash, when he expressed the desire to buy a Zen, he told Satyavrat that he won't settle for a second-hand car this time. "I want a new car," he told Satyavrat.

The Zen was registered in the name of one Rajeshwar Pradhan of Gorakhpur. Anand also bought a Royal Enfield Bullet in the name of one Arvind. He stocked number plates of UP, Bihar, Haryana and Delhi to be used at different times.

One day, at around 10 a.m., the man called PP Singh. "Some people are here. They came in a Zen," he said. The information came to us.

The colony had three exits. We separated ourselves into three teams to guard all three. Satyendra Vir Singh and Tevatiya were at the first, sub-inspector Parashar and I at the second and Avinash and others stood at the third entry. Everyone kept in touch with each other through wireless.

We were informed that the man was getting into the car. We were ready. The Zen exited from the gate where Satyendra Vir Singh was present with Tevatiya. They followed it. We were also told that the car was going towards Ghaziabad.

All our vehicles began following them. Parashar and I got close to the Zen. The man in it was driving slowly and talking on a mobile phone. We overtook him and yanked him out of the car before he could react and put him in our Tata Sumo.

Others also came. We asked him to identify himself. First, he gave us some names, but when we became strict with him, he said he was Anand Pandey.

Lucknow had to be informed. We told the officers that he was probably Shriprakash, but was giving us the wrong name. We asked him about the AK-47. We told him that Ladhani had told us about a pistol. Where was that?

Anand told us that he used ten lakh rupees to buy a Zen and a Bullet. He also told us about buying a flat. The remaining money, he said, was with Satyavrat in Lucknow. He said the AK-47 was also in Lucknow. We didn't believe him. He wasn't revealing much. It was getting dark and we were frustrated with him.

"I feel it will be right to shoot him dead," Satyendra Vir Singh suggested. He got jittery at the mention of killing someone.

"Take me to the slums near Narula's – the AK-47 is there," he said.

The trick had worked. We went to the slums. He pointed to a single-storey house. "When you knock, a woman will open the door. Go to the second room. The AK-47 is under the bed in a bag," he said.

Satyendra Vir Singh and Tevatiya went inside the house. The others waited with him in the car. They found the AK-47 along with a hundred cartridges wrapped in a polythene packet. The house was searched in the hope of finding the ransom money, but we didn't find anything else.

We became certain that he was either Shriprakash or Anand. We wanted to recover the money by hook or by crook. "*Paisa kahan hai bata de, warna goli mar denge* (Tell us where the money is or we will shoot you)," we were threatening him. It must have been seven in the evening.

Suddenly, he sprang from the middle seat and jumped out of the Tata Sumo. He must have thought that we would kill him and he wanted to escape. When he was running, he hit something and fell. Parashar and I got to him. He tried to snatch our pistol. When he failed, he began running again.

A shot was fired. He fell. It was dark and we didn't know where he had been hit.

We also thought it was important to inform the Delhi Police. When a team arrived, we went closer to check on him. Anand Pandey was dead. It was 14 December 1997.

The next morning, details of the AK-47 were circulated among the agencies. The CBI SP who had investigated the Purulia arms drop case said that the gun was indeed from that lot. He also got interested in the case. His interest was limited to finding out how a Purulia weapon got to this gang. We shared with him all the information that we had about the gang and its background.

We had found a diary from Anand, which led to the recovery of the ransom money.

It was time for us to return to Lucknow. The next day, when we assembled for stock taking, we felt dismayed that we were clueless about the split between Shriprakash and Anand. We had been thinking that Shriprakash kidnapped Ladhani, but it was done by Anand. The informers, who would tip us off about the gang, shared information as if they had been with them the previous evening. All of them claimed to be privy to inside information, but none of them reported this very important development. Both

Shriprakash and Anand had strong firepower; Sudhir was with them in all operations, but he mostly handled the logistics and drove them around.

The newspapers wrote about the encounter of Anand Pandey and the recovery of an AK-47. However, they didn't fail to point out that we hadn't been able to get to Shriprakash. Such news reports and editorial comments were disheartening; what was more disturbing was the fact that the senior officers, especially those in the police headquarters, were also acerbic.

"*Aisa kya teer mar diya* (What greatness have you achieved)?" they would mock us. "*Jise pakadna hai, wo to aap logon ko milta nahin* (The person whom you should arrest is still roaming free)." These comments threw a pall over our efforts and were very discouraging.

But they only stated a fact. A fact that gnawed all of us – Shriprakash was still out there, roaming freely.

Chapter 11
The Rastogi Kidnapping

Shriprakash was greedy, not only for money, but also for fame. He yearned for fame and never shied away from taking the blame for a crime he had committed. He would monitor newspapers to keep himself updated about what the journalists were writing about him, his gang and its reign of terror. He used to get upset if the newspaper played down his savagery. The flunkeys in Lucknow, who made kundalis, would update him about what had been published. He wanted the newspapers to "certify" his escapades. He would go to any extent to get validation. The lengthier the news piece would be, the more gratified he felt.

After the killing of Anand Pandey, he called the newspapers.

"I have killed Anand Pandey. Death is the only punishment for people who betray me," he said.

"Who is this?"

"Who else can I be? Shriprakash Shukla," he thundered. "That bastard decamped with my AK-47."

The woman on the other end of the conversation froze. The name made her tongue-tied.

He continued, "I didn't kill him myself because he was an old associate; had been with me in several operations and was beside me during my bad days. Naturally, I didn't want to dirty my hands with his blood, but he had to face punishment. I tipped off the police about his location."

"Okay..." The woman didn't know what to say. Before she could gather her thoughts, the call ended.

Along with fame, this was also Shriprakash's way of sending out a message to members of his gang to stay loyal. He always suspected them of being a police mole.

Anuj Pratap Singh filled in the void left by Anand's exit. But he was not onboarded easily. He had to undergo a battery of tests to prove his loyalty. Anuj could well have been someone's plant in the gang. Rajan Tiwari, Satyavrat Rai and Bhuwar Rai had sided with Anand. Rajan Pradhan had got him a car and a motorcycle. He had also helped him shift his family. They all had rooted for Anand. Shriprakash doubted Anuj could be one of Anand's men. After the indoctrination, Anuj got into the gang.

The core group now comprised Shriprakash, Sudhir and Anuj.

Shriprakash tried to be vainglorious by calling newspapers, but he was crippled from inside, worrying about how the police had got to Anand. The Mokama raid had already unnerved him, but this was bigger and graver. If they could get Anand, they could get him too, he thought.

But how? "The gang uses mobile phones. The police can't tap these and find out locations based on phone conversations. No one would ever dare to provide any information about the gang to the police. Where is the leak?" He would often speak his mind with Sudhir and Anuj, sounding concerned about how the leak could be plugged.

They went to Nepal for some time and when they returned, they felt the need to shake things up and reorganize themselves. They needed money for that. Shriprakash said he would ask

Surajbhan for one more AK-47. He also felt the need to have a safe place in Nepal, a house or a hotel, for them to escape whenever needed. He preferred hotels because it was easier to slip out of hotels during police raids than it was from private houses. He put his contacts in Nepal on the job of locating one such hotel. Preferably in Viratnagar. He liked that place very much.

Meanwhile, police pressure was increasing in Gorakhpur. In Lucknow too, the police were trying to get to the gang and neutralise it. In Mokama, the police found his pistol and car. They were close. Shriprakash was worried - probably for the first time after starting in the underworld.

The police were also under pressure. True, Anand had been a big success, but the senior police officers and people in the government were not content. Also, the special unit formed to nab Shriprakash was without an office.

The search took the team to Vigyanpuri, a colony of police officers, serving and retired. The house of a deputy SP, who retired from the Forensic Science Laboratory in Mahanagar, was deserted. The officer who used to live in the house died a tragic death. He belonged to Punjab but settled down here after retirement. He lived alone. He died in solitude; the body was recovered seven days later. The neighbours called the police when a fetid stench shrouded the entire area. The police performed his last rites.

One day, Shriram Arun called me. I was posted as CO Mahanagar at that time. He informed me that someone was doing some construction here. We went to the spot. The man showed some documents, but they looked fake. We sealed the house and registered an FIR against him on charges of forgery.

Chacha Zaidi, the former SDM, was famously called so in Lucknow. He was the SDM even after fifteen years of retirement. He was in charge of duties for the 26 January parade, Moharram procession and other important events. An experienced and old hand, he got government vehicles, wireless sets, etc., from successive governments. It cannot be said for sure whether he was reemployed instead of pay minus pension or his service was extended. He was a native of Jaunpur and was a very hard-working man. He was ACM-6 and the Mahanagar area was under his jurisdiction.

We gave him a report and told him that someone was trying to take possession of the house. We stopped the activity and booked that person under section 420 IPC. The SDM sent his men to check records, and after he was satisfied that the house had no claimant, he passed an order under IPC 145 to hand it over to the police.

We went to Ajay Raj Sharma and told him about the house. "No one is willing to rent their house to us. We already have possession of this one. This is our best shot!"

He agreed and offered to give us ₹50,000 for its upkeep.

The notification for the special unit was out. Along with the primary intention to put an end to the reign of Shriprakash's terror, the unit had some other agenda points as well, such as arms smuggling. The unit was named the Special Task Force.

After getting a green signal from ADG LO, OP Tripathi and Malviya were tasked with the job of getting the house ready. They had been inspectors in Lucknow earlier. They got labourers to clean the house. An electrician was called to fix electric points and wiring. Some men were called to whitewash the walls. The house became ready in a matter of four days.

It was decided to inaugurate the STF office on 4 May. ADG LO would do the honours. We called a priest to perform the auspicious ceremony of breaking a coconut. This was done to take blessings from the Almighty before the commencement of work. The house was being used for a special purpose, so we wanted it to be duly inaugurated.

People who know Ajay Raj Sharma would remember that he was a bulky man but very sporty and energetic. He captained the cricket team of IPS officers in Uttar Pradesh till the time he was in the state cadre. Although he was the *jajmaan* during the inauguration ceremony and was supposed to sit on the floor, but because of his weight, he found it inconvenient and needed a chair. The office was inaugurated but only one room was fit for work. It was cramped. Tables and chairs from a tent house filled it. The STF had an office now.

A telephone line, a stenographer and a computer were immediate needs. Arun Kumar managed to get a disconnected telephone number of FSL transferred to our office. Shamin, who had been with him when he was SSP Bareilly and whose family lived in Lucknow too, was transferred as Arun Kumar's stenographer. When we went to the Usha and Essar offices to get CDRs, we would be deluged with 600 to 700 pages for one mobile number. The staff said, "It is such a waste of stationery. Why don't you get a computer? We can transfer these pages on email and save paper. It will also make analysis easier." Manual dissection was tedious; the computer could do that in a jiffy. But the problem was that no one in the STF knew how to use computers. We got the jitters at the mere mention of the word "computer".

Although it is a digression, but policemen's dalliance with

computers is an amusing story. When I was CO Hazratganj, the first internet connection was taken for the office of DIG Range, Kashmir Singh. After a month, when the bill arrived, it was an exorbitant ₹20,000. The DIG got alarmed. He said he had not used the internet even for a moment, then how could it be billed so much? Obviously, people in his office were surfing it for their carnal appetites but when the bill amount became an issue, no one owned up. Every office has some *gyanchands*, people who seem to have a solution for every problem. One gyanchand in the DIG office suggested that the police must lodge an FIR for theft of data. A case under section 379 was indeed registered at Hazratganj Kotwali by the staff officer of the DIG. Not too many people in the police, especially at the police-station level, were conversant with the IT Act.

Coming back to our story, the STF office now had a telephone and a stenographer, but it needed vehicles as well. The Haridwar kumbh mela - which is a huge gathering of devotees - had ended. The three vehicles UP Police had purchased during the congregation - one Ambassador and two jeeps - were up for grabs. The DGP ordered the vehicles to be given to the STF. However, the jeeps could not match the speed of cars used by these criminals. Plus, we needed a vehicle that had room for five to six people. We did a market survey and found that the recently launched Tata Sumo fitted the bill.

Generally, it is very difficult to go for something which is not the norm while making a government purchase. The norm at that time was to have Mahindra vehicles. But luckily, the ADG pulled strings and got us ten Tata Sumos. The STF also got sophisticated weapons like pistols, AK-47 and revolvers. It was decided that our weapons would be stored in the armory of 35 PAC. The STF was to not have any overlap with the district police.

All this happened within a span of about fifteen days of the formation of the STF but the force itself was tiny - it had only seventeen policemen. People were disinterested in joining a new unit - that too a unit whose primary aim was to eliminate the deadliest gangster of that time.

It took us some time to adjust to the new office. Furniture was rented and the seating plan was decided. The offices of the DGP and the SSP treated us like shunted people - like leftovers. Everyone was sceptical about our success. "*Yeh pakdenge Shriprakash ko* (These men will arrest Shriprakash)!" they would sneer in private.

The media didn't allow us a honeymoon period. They became scathing from the day the STF was formed. It's a group of rejected officers, they would write, often calling the force a white elephant. Shriprakash had committed one horrendous crime after the other. The district police had looked lily-livered and here was a special force that people doubted.

Amidst this, twenty days after the inauguration of the STF office, Shriprakash struck again. Kunal Rastogi, the son of a prominent wholesale supplier of medicines, Kamal Krishna Rastogi, was kidnapped from Gokhale Marg.

Shriprakash had become desperate for funds after Anand's killing to expand and secure his gang. He had surveyed some old kundalis and got new ones prepared. The Lucknow men had been activated. They had come to Shriprakash with the kundali of Kamal Krishna Rastogi or KK Rastogi, as the man was called.

Shriprakash repeated his usual modus operandi – the man was called and his day's activities sprinkled with minute details were narrated to him. Rastogi didn't get terrified. Some more calls were made to Rastogi. One day, he told Shriprakash bluntly that he won't give him a penny.

"My heydays are over. There was a time when my firm Solomon & Solomon was the only agency in Lucknow supplying medicines to not only UP but also all of north India. But now there's competition. I don't make much profit," he told Shriprakash in exasperation.

The man who made the kundali said Rastogi could easily shell out a crore. "*Bahut property hai, bahut paisa hai,*" he informed Shriprakash.

Shriprakash flew into a rage at Rastogi's temerity. "How dare you refuse me? You will pay for this audacity soon!" He told Sudhir and Anuj to get ready to kidnap either the father or the son.

Rastogi went for morning walks to the botanical garden with his son Kunal from their house on Gokhale Marg. Shriprakash and his aides waited for them near their house. When they came out of their house, the gang chased them. The gang overtook them in their white Maruti 800. Rastogi was driving the car. He rammed the Maruti but due to the impact, the door on the driver's side got locked. Shriprakash got off his car and pumped five bullets into Rastogi's head without uttering a single word. Before Kunal could react, he was dragged out and plunked into the Maruti.

They took Kunal to a house in Indira Nagar. It belonged to a leather trader from Kanpur. We later got to know that this trader's name was Mr Upadhyay. He had placed an advertisement in the local papers for a tenant for his house. Anuj got in touch with him.

When Upadhyay said he would rent it to only a family, Anuj told him that his brother and his family would come from Gorakhpur after the kid's exam was over. He got the house.

It was a furnished, two-storey house. They parked the Maruti, covered it and took Kunal inside. Rastogi was the head of the family, but he had been killed. The second male member, Kunal, was in captivity.

This incident caused a massive uproar. Rajiv Ratan Shah, the then principal secretary (home), called an urgent meeting and said it had now become unbearable. There were protests by trade organisations and *vyapar mandals*. The business community was frightened by this ghastly event. The then Lucknow DM, Sada Kant, had to announce that the process of issuing arms licenses would be expedited. He also said that businessmen who had gun licenses will be given arms training in the police line from 15 July 1998.

Businessmen were already getting Shriprakash's phone calls. Some of them paid him discreetly without reporting it to the police. Nonetheless, they were all terrified. The Rastogi murder and kidnapping spooked them further.

In a matter of days, the ransom calls began. Shriprakash asked for two crore rupees. He was aware that Kunal's in-laws were big jewellers in Kanpur. He asked the family to tell them to pay.

Shriprakash called two men from Gorakhpur to look after Kunal. They got him some clothes. Having lost his father, Kunal was in a terrible state, but the gang didn't let him talk to his mother or wife. He also had an aunt who was closest to the family. When the police went to Rastogi's house, she and her husband did the talking.

The family was shattered – Shriprakash had described to them how he had killed Rastogi and how he was planning to eliminate Kunal if he did not get the money. Kunal was the only son; the family, his in-laws, relatives and people from the community didn't want any harm to befall him.

Then the calls stopped coming. Everyone got worried that probably Kunal had been killed, but the fact was that Shriprakash, Sudhir and Anuj had gone to Mokama, leaving Kunal in the Indira Nagar house.

The ransom negotiations were going on when one day, Shriprakash got a call from Mokama. Surajbhan had summoned him for some urgent work. "Dada wants you here as soon as possible," the caller said. When Shriprakash told him that he had a tender, the man said he could delegate someone to look after it. "It is in your custody, you will get it back sooner or later; this is more important," he said.

Shriprakash sensed the urgency in his tone and agreed to travel. But not before getting another tender.

Shriprakash told his gang members that it was unclear from the call how many days they would require to be in Mokama and proposed another kidnapping. "We will keep the second tender on the first floor of the house," he said.

Sudhir brought out the kundali of one cloth merchant who had a Raymond showroom in Hazratganj. The flunkeys were asked to refresh it with the latest activities. They got to work and an updated kundali was ready by the evening.

"If he pays, very well. Otherwise, we will pick him too and dump him here. We will keep negotiating from Mokama and collect the ransom on our return," Shriprakash told the gang.

The routine phone calls began. Shriprakash called the man. "Lala, I have called so many times. Don't you get it? Do you wish to die?" he barked. He provided the man with details of his day's activities. "Did you have a good time with your father at the showroom? Well, that is going to get over soon!"

Shriprakash continued, "Your father wore a black shirt and white trousers, and you were in a pink check shirt and black trousers. Around 11.30 a.m., a minister came to your shop with his family to buy presents for his daughter's wedding. After an hour, when they were leaving, you came out to see them off. After they left, you were alone. You know what, I could have turned your head into a brass factory, but I thought maybe you will be wise."

Shriprakash also narrated the details of what the man did at Malhotra paan shop near the stadium. "I was there too. You were staring at Death in its face. Then two people came to you. One of them, a short person, took you aside towards the State Bank of India to discuss something..."

"Tell me what to do," the businessman interposed, sweating with fear.

"You decide today whether you want to pay or achieve *moksha* at Bhainsakund. Keep fifty lakh rupees ready by tomorrow."

"*Itna kaisa ho payega* (How can this much money be arranged)?" Lala said meekly. "I don't have this much money. I know I cannot escape you, but I really don't have this much."

Shriprakash told him to think overnight. "I will call you at nine tomorrow morning. Take a decision – whether you want to be killed or give me money," he said and slammed the phone down.

The businessman's wife had heard the conversation. "Who was it? Why are you sweating?" she asked. He told her that Shriprakash Shukla had called.

"*Arrey baap re! Wo to bahut bada gunda hai* (Oh my goodness! He is a dangerous gangster). There are reports about him in the newspapers every day. But why is he asking you for money?" she didn't understand that it was an extortion call. When the husband told her about the "goonda tax", she suggested that he should talk to Moolraj Arora. "People say that Shriprakash talks to him. He may help you," she said.

The businessman dialled Arora. He was already fed up with calls from Shriprakash. "I got out of his clutches by paying money. He keeps calling for more. Keep me out of this please," Moolraj sounded helpless. He said he was in fact planning to leave Lucknow to escape the criminal.

The wife then suggested that he should report the call to the SSP. "Take some business leaders with you. He will surely provide you with police protection," she said.

The businessman said Moolraj Arora told him that when Shriprakash was taking him to Bihar, he thought the police would stop them at checkpoints and he would get time to raise an alarm, but that didn't happen. The police saluted him and offered him free passage. Arora suspected he had setting from top to bottom in the police and that's why they don't touch him.

"All right then. Can you then tell him to fix your competitors? Either take money from them or get their showrooms closed?" The wife kept thinking of ways to get out of the precarious condition.

"This is nonsense," the businessman said. "When did you become so selfish? Moreover, the police will find this out and we will both be in jail. Those shopkeepers also have families. They may be my competitor, but is it right to throw them under the bus?!"

The next morning, as the family waited for the dreaded call, the wife said she would handle it. "I will say you have gone for a bath and try to smooth-talk him into sparing us," she said.

The phone rang.

"Who's this?" the wife asked.

"Who are YOU? Where's Lala?"

She said he was waiting for someone's phone and has gone to take a bath. "Tell me who you are. I will tell him when he returns," she said.

"When I told him that I will call at nine, he should have waited."

"Tell me who you are. I will tell him when he returns," she repeated.

"Ashok Singh," came the voice from the other end.

"Oh, bhai sa'ab, I think he was waiting for you only," she said and bawled pleadingly. "We have small children. *Hum waise nahin hain jaisa aap samajh rahe hain* (We are not rich as you think we are). Have mercy on us."

"Really?" He sneered. "As if I don't know about the kilos of gold that you were shamelessly flaunting when you went to the birthday party two days ago. After looting the entire city, you want me to have mercy on you?"

She was dumbfounded. The businessman was standing close to her, overhearing the conversation.

Shriprakash continued, "I don't want to talk to you. Why did you answer?"

The wife was still at a loss for words when he asked, "What is your name?"

"Bhagyashree," she bleated.

"That's a lovely name! If you were a tad taller, you would have been Lucknow's most beautiful woman," he said with a slurp.

The receiver fell from her hand. The businessman put it back on the cradle. When she gained her composure, she said, "He is a dangerous man. We will have to pay him." She asked her husband to negotiate hard. "Let's pay him the least we can," she said and recalled how he even knew about the birthday party that the family attended a few days ago. She wondered aloud that either someone close to them was feeding him with the information or he was actually following them.

The phone rang again.

"I told you to wait for my call. Why did you go for a bath?" Shriprakash roared after hearing the businessman's voice. "You thought I would fall for your wife's guile?"

The businessman saw no point in labouring the conversation. "*Bhaiyya, fifty lakh nahi ho payega* (We cannot afford fifty lakh)."

"How much can you give me then?" Shriprakash asked.

"Five lakhs," he said almost inaudibly.

"Five lakhs?" Shriprakash hollered, cussing loudly.

He was foul-mouthed and used very distinct curse words. So distinct that while hearing tapes of phone recordings, we could tell it was Shriprakash without even looking at the stickers.

The businessman told him that there were three more shops, and the business wasn't good as it once used to be. Shriprakash demanded to know the names of the other businessmen. The businessman named them in one breath.

"Don't worry about business," Shriprakash had cooled down. "You pay me and I will make sure that you have a good business. *Hazratganj me chamka doonga tujhe* (You will be a shining star in Hazratganj). I know those three - two Sindhis and one baniya. One of them, who is very fair, is a sweet talker but very crooked. I know that. I will get their showrooms shut. You will have a monopoly."

The businessman said he didn't want the showrooms to close. "I can give you five lakhs now and pay the remaining amount in installments over a year," he said.

Shriprakash got angry again. The abuses followed. But then he said, "Okay, keep five lakhs ready at the counter tomorrow; I will send someone to collect it."

Shriprakash thought to himself that he had planned to kidnap him, but he had agreed to pay and had even provided information about three prospective tenders. He felt satisfied.

He told his gang that they would collect five lakhs the next day before leaving for Mokama. "We may need this money during the journey," he said.

A prominent Hazratganj businessman collected the money and delivered it to the gang at a place near Chinhat.

They went to Mokama the next day.

Chapter 12
Murder in a Hospital

The next day, upon reaching Surajbhan in Bihar, Shriprakash told Surajbhan about Kunal, who was in his custody. "I wanted to dispose of the tender, but you said there was some urgent work, so here we are," he said.

They discussed Anand's encounter. Surajbhan said he got killed because he parted ways. Shriprakash knew they were more powerful when they stayed together. "I know. But what is done is done, bhai," Shriprakash said. "Right now, I need money to reorganize myself in Anand's absence."

Soon, Surajbhan got down to brass tacks.

Brij Bihari Prasad, the second-in-command in the Bihar government, was planning to get Surajbhan out of his way. He believed Surajbhan's men had tipped off the CBI or helped the agency in the investigation of a case in which he was named in the charge sheet. Prasad was very close to Lalu Prasad Yadav, the then chief minister, but had to be dropped from the cabinet after the CBI charges. Devendra Dubey, the MLA, had been killed. Among the three brothers - Chhutkun, Butkun and Munna - only Munna was alive. These were Surajbhan's friends who had helped him eliminate his adversaries. Brij Bihari Prasad was the main suspect in the Devendra Dubey murder case. He was a very powerful minister and in Bihar, FIRs in political murders are so convoluted that most people go scot-free.

Surajbhan and Brij Bihari Prasad were baying for each other's blood. After the CBI charge sheet, Prasad had got himself admitted to Indira Gandhi Institute of Medical Sciences (IGIMS) in Patna. Even though he ceased to be a minister, his clout remained and he held *durbars* in the hospital every day.

When Shriprakash heard Brij Bihari Prasad's name, he also got cold feet. He was a very powerful man and a close aide of the current chief minister.

"Ashok Singh, there's no one, except you, who can do this for me," Surajbhan said. "We need to finish him in the hospital itself."

Shriprakash didn't want to let Surajbhan down. He said, "I need some time to understand the situation."

"I don't have too much time in my hand. That's why I have called you urgently to Mokama, even though there was a tender to be disposed of."

Surajbhan told him that there was a doctor in IGIMS who belonged to Mokama. "I will call him. You go and meet him and figure how you could get close to Brij Bihari Prasad in the hospital," he said. "You need to do the recce within ten days. Brij Bihari is safe in the hospital, but I may not be alive."

As soon as Surajbhan uttered these words, everyone in the room froze. The room became so silent that you could hear a pin drop. "No dada, nothing will happen to you. Let me start working on this from tomorrow itself," Shriprakash said to reassure Surajbhan.

Surajbhan smiled in optimism.

"We need to prepare his kundali. He must be surrounded by a large number of Rahus and Ketus."

"I know the Rahu and Ketu thing," Surajbhan said with a mild laugh.

"It's foolhardy to embark on a mission without the knowledge of them, you know."

"I agree. If what I know is right, Rahu is a small weapon, and Ketu, big ones, right?"

"Ji dada," Shriprakash answered. "We need to know how many of those are with the target, how many on the left, and how many on the right; how many behind him and also in the front. Until we have the full kundali, we don't take the plunge."

The next day, Shriprakash was in the OPD of IGIMS. The Mokama doctor was a simple man. He had already heard from Surajbhan and was a little nervous. Shriprakash asked him where Brij Bihari was admitted. The doctor said that he needed to find out, but first, he needed to get Shriprakash admitted.

"A doctor needs to suggest admission. Then we will go to a private ward. Do you have any medical history?" the OPD doctor asked Shriprakash.

He was blank. The doctor suggested he tell the consultant that he has a problem of rapid heartbeat. "Tell him that sometimes your heart beats very fast. You get palpitations and sweat. They will admit you and put you through to a lot of tests. This will require you to stay at the hospital for at least eight to ten days. During this time, you can work on your mission."

An OPD ticket was made. The doctor wrote tachycardia with a query and referred Shriprakash to a cardiologist.

The cardiologist examined him and said he looked normal. Shriprakash said he may be normal now, but when his heart would beat rapidly, he sweats profusely and gets darkness before his eyes. "*Aankho ke saamne tare nachne lagte hain* (I see stars during these episodes)," he said.

The doctor said he would require to be admitted.

"Okay, doctor sa'ab. Whatever you suggest," Shriprakash said without giving even a hint of his plan.

"Have you come prepared?"

"Yes, I have," Shriprakash said.

"We will do some tests. The treatment will start only after we have the test reports in hand and have diagnosed the problem."

In the meanwhile, Sudhir and Anuj had made enquiries and found out which ward Brij Bihari Prasad was admitted in.

They came back to the doctor in the OPD. "He's sent him to the general ward," Sudhir said, "but we need Shriprakash in the private ward on the same floor as that of Brij Bihari Prasad."

The doctor made some calls and managed to send them to the private ward. The floor on which Brij Bihari's ward was located had been vacated. Ten gun-wielding men guarded the entry. The floor was out of bounds for patients and outsiders. There was a room for the VIP visitors who came to ask after Brij Bihari Prasad. For the common men, he would come downstairs and hold a durbar in the hospital lawn. Fifteen to twenty armed men guarded him during these public appearances.

The Mokama doctor tried for a room on that particular floor. He told the hospital administration that the patient had come to him through a recommendation of someone very important.

They got a room close to Brij Bihari's room. Sudhir looked around and felt satisfied with the location of the room. "Bhaiyya, we can keep a watch on him from here. We will also chat up people who come to visit him."

Sudhir bought a pillow, some bed sheets, a water jug and a glass – things that one needs in a hospital room. The weapons were kept in bags and hidden under the bed. He was keen that the "pakad" be disposed of but Shriprakash said, "*Dada ka kaam hai, karna zaroori hai* (It's Dada's work. We have to finish it). If you don't do his work, we will have a problem in the future."

Hospital staff started taking his samples for various tests. Sudhir and Anuj were doing the recce. They befriended some security men who told them that the minister – they still called him that – didn't meet commoners in the room. Only ministers or VIPs were allowed there.

The gang decided to execute the operation when Brij Bihari Prasad was surrounded by his followers in the lawn. They rehearsed.

Shriprakash wrapped a blanket around himself and came down under the pretence of taking a walk. Doctors recommend this for some patients, especially the infirm. They took rounds of the lawn, taking mental notes about the security paraphernalia with the leader. There were about twelve private security guards with rifles, eight to ten policemen with smaller weapons and one security personnel had a Sten gun. Shriprakash and his men were calculating in their head about the shortest distance to the boundary wall from where they could jump over after shooting the politician dead and escape in cars waiting on the other side.

They took three rounds – Shriprakash needed time to plan. Some people asked why such a young man was in the hospital. The attendants, Sudhir and Anuj, said the patient had a heart problem and needed to be operated on. "Three days ago, he had a paralytic attack too. He can't walk properly. Doctors have told him to walk twice a day so that his vitals are good before the surgery," they told the curious people.

"*Tch, tch*! This is no age to have a heart operation," some of them said, sympathising with the patient.

Shriprakash returned to the hospital room. "I would be soaked in sweat with this darn blanket," he said, flinging it off. "We will have to kill him in the first round itself. My blanket may drop or someone may notice a change in my gait. That will be disastrous - didn't you see the firepower around Brij Bihari?" he shot the question at Sudhir and Anuj.

They were getting desperate for the operation because Kunal was held captive in Lucknow. They would routinely call their men to find out how he was behaving. The men reported that he was doing quite well and never tried to escape. "He cries all day," they told Sudhir. "He's been wearing the same undergarments for more than twenty days and wants to change them."

Shriprakash told the men to bring new undergarments for him. "Ask him his size and get them for him, but from Chinhat or Mahanagar - the police dogs must be sniffing around so don't go to a nearby market."

It was 13 June 1998. Shriprakash wrapped a blanket and came downstairs with Anuj in tow, holding the saline water bottle. Sudhir followed with the bag of weapons and went straight to the toilet on the ground floor near the lawn. Shriprakash looked dishevelled and emaciated. He also went to the toilet. It was decided that if someone else came to use the facility while they were tucking the pistols into their trousers, they would say that a very sick patient was inside and that they should wait until he had used the toilet.

Shriprakash took the AK-47 and a .45mm pistol under the blanket. Sudhir and Anuj also took their weapons.

Meanwhile, two vehicles had pulled up on the other side of the boundary wall. There were armed men in the vehicles. If Shriprakash failed, these men would offer them cover fire to facilitate the escape. Surajbhan and his cousin Lallan Singh were in those cars.

Brij Bihari emerged with his band of security men surrounding him. He sat on a chair. His followers were fawning over their leader.

Shriprakash took one round. As he started the second, he walked closer to Brij Bihari Prasad, slung the blanket on the lawn and pulled the trigger of the assault rifle. The AK-47 spewed fire into the politician's body. Brij Bihari Prasad collapsed. Everyone ran helter-skelter. The security guards and the policemen dashed into the hospital building for cover.

Sudhir and Anuj also fired from their pistols. Then the three leaped towards the boundary wall, jumped over and crossed it.

The two cars soon started moving. About five minutes later, they heard gunshots from the hospital. Sudhir looked puzzled.

"Don't worry, it's perfunctory," Shriprakash said explaining to Sudhir and Anuj why there were firings. "Read in the newspapers tomorrow. These must be the policemen. This is to save their skins. When the senior officers descend on the crime scene, these cops will tell them that they ran after the attackers, even opened fire at them - the stories that they cook to escape disciplinary action for failing to protect a VIP are sometimes hilarious."

Surajbhan was ecstatic. He patted Shriprakash on the back and said only he could have done it. "Dada, as I said, the person who fires the first bullet is the king in such situations. Even if the other person has fifty guns with him, it's no use," Shriprakash said.

Sudhir said when they were escaping, he had turned to see if they were being chased and found that the policemen were still missing, maybe too scared to emerge out of their hideout. Even the private guards had disappeared - some after abandoning their rifles.

Shriprakash carried the conversation forward. "There's never danger from policemen; it's the private security guards who sometimes take the risk and open a front. Policemen guarding VIPs are the first ones to scoot when the person they are providing security to comes under attack."

Shriprakash then told Surajbhan that they will stop at an eatery outside Patna. "Please send our car there. We will leave from here as soon as possible."

Surajbhan thanked them profusely once again before they bid goodbye. The man thought his field was now clear with all his opponents eliminated; if there are any left, they will fall in line after this big murder.

Shriprakash and the gang reached the eatery and they waited for their car. They rejoiced their victory and laughed at how the security men and the police abandoned Brij Bihari Prasad when he needed them the most.

"Bhaiyya, will this end somewhere?" Sudhir asked pensively.

"This is a battle for supremacy, Sudhir. Without dada, we cannot fight this. We need weapons and we don't have as many as dada has. We need at least five more AK-47s. We will talk to dada about it. Our only rival now is Hari Shankar Tiwari and we will fix him soon," Shriprakash replied.

"But, what next?"

"Next is absolute control over Lucknow. We need a constant source of income. We will set the vyapar mandal leaders right first. They hold protests and close markets. When they are in their place, the businessmen will not think twice before giving us money."

"They give money even now."

"Not like this. It should be smooth. We should not need to call them repeatedly and give them so much time. It should be like *jisko phone kar do, wo aakar paisa de de* (It should be like whosoever gets a call should come and give us the money)."

"Is that possible?"

"Of course! They give money to corporators, MLAs, vyapar mandal leaders, sales tax, police, small-time politicians... All the people we have called have mentioned that they give a lot of money already to them. We will stop this business once and for all. All the money should come to us."

Shriprakash had lofty ideas. "When we snap supply of police, politicians, officers, they will become restless. They will wring the businessmen. *Samjhana padega, warna khopdi me goli utar di jayegi* (They have to understand this or else bullets will be pumped in their heads). That's the way to establish your reign of terror. They should come running to you with money when you tell them."

He then opened the cards that Sudhir and Anuj were unaware of.

"When we have made money, dada and I have decided to

field our candidates in elections. Imagine if we have ten to fifteen MLAs each. Then no government can be formed without our support. We will be the kingmakers," he said.

"Won't that require a lot of money?" Sudhir continued to sound incredulous.

"Money we will amass. These businessmen fund rallies, meetings and bring people to political events. People, you see, are daily-wage workers. They will shout *zindabad murdabad* for anyone who pays them."

Meanwhile, the car arrived. They drove to Lucknow and reached late at night. Everything was all right at the Indira Nagar house where they had held Kunal captive.

Shriprakash spoke to him. "It's been about a month. Tell your family to pay, otherwise I will kill you. We cannot wait endlessly."

Negotiations began. Kunal's in-laws brokered the ransom amount. The money was paid in a Faizabad hotel owned by a former MP from Ambedkar Nagar.

Brij Bihar Prasad's killing had major repercussions. The closest man of the chief minister had been killed in the middle of the town. That too in broad daylight. In cold blood. The man had been dropped from the cabinet after an indictment by the CBI, but he still was a very powerful man in Bihar politics.

When the police in Patna figured that Shriprakash was behind the murder, they contacted us – the UP STF.

We were put up in a forest guesthouse near Patna zoo. The officers said we had been chasing Shriprakash, had killed Anand

Pandey and raided Mokama. "You might be identified, so we will keep you in the guest house. People will come to you to brief you about the investigation or the leads, but please don't step out."

We were there for a couple of days. Everyone knew that Surajbhan would lead us on to Shriprakash, but the Bihar Police could not lay their hands on him. Meanwhile, we collected numbers, investigated the hospital and found out about the Mokama doctor. But the government was sensitive about doctors. It said we could confront a doctor only if we had concrete information. Otherwise, they would call for a strike. Doctors' strike in IGIMS would cripple medical services and would bring the government on its knees, we were told.

We returned to Lucknow without questioning the Mokama doctor thoroughly. We could not churn out any leads about Shriprakash from him.

We were in awe of Shriprakash's effrontery – he held a man captive, yet he agreed to travel for this big political murder.

This wasn't all. IG Patna spoke to Arun Kumar about another escapade. When Shriprakash was in the hospital, he bumped into a resident doctor a couple of times in the chamber of the Mokama doctor. He started inquiring about her. Surajbhan's men also tried to get information about her, but without success.

Pappu Yadav was an affluent politician. It was found that she was either Pappu Yadav's sister or someone related to him. But it didn't matter to Shriprakash. He went ahead and accosted the lady resident doctor. She told him that she was Pappu Yadav's sister, thinking that the name would shoot him away. But Shriprakash was a dreaded gangster.

"Tell him my name – Shriprakash Shukla," he told her. He also called Pappu Yadav and let fly with a stream of abuses.

The IG was worried Pappu Yadav could be next.

Pappu Yadav contacted the STF SSP too. He said Shriprakash had crossed all limits and only the STF was capable of showing him his real place. "I am ready to extend all help. He had created terror even among the bahubalis," he told the SSP.

Shriprakash was in the habit of stalking women. He would get their telephone numbers and talk rubbish to them. The pervert that he was.

Meanwhile, Shriprakash became a big name in Bihar's crime circle too. People knew that he worked for Surajbhan, had strong firepower and was extremely daring.

Nine people, including Surajbhan, Lallan Singh and two MLAs, were named in the Brij Bihari Prasad murder FIR.

The murder changed the political landscape of Bihar. It was the time of bahubalis in politics. The wannabes found this a shortcut to enter politics. They thought the bigger the criminal, the better the chance of a political party fielding them in elections.

After Brij Bihari's murder, the Bihar Police also started chasing Shriprakash. Once there was an encounter in which Surajbhan was hit in the leg. His men couldn't bring him to Lucknow or Gorakhpur for treatment. The wound continued to get complicated.

Dhirendra Singh's cousin, Dr Anil Singh, ran a hospital named City Hospital in Allahabad. Surajbhan was taken there. The wound improved. But the Bihar Police got a whiff of this and passed the information to us. When we raided the hospital,

Surajbhan had left. We never got to know if he was tipped off about the raid and fled or he was discharged from the hospital.

Shriprakash started claiming flamboyantly that he was the undisputed leader of the crime world. He began owning even small crimes as he called the newspaper offices. If crime reporters took a divergent line or wrote about other gangs, he even threatened them. None of the newspaper managements reported this to the police out of fear. Shriprakash won't hesitate in killing reporters, they thought.

Shriprakash was then spotted at Gomti Motors. He was getting a Jonga painted. It was built by the Vehicle Factory Jabalpur, a unit of Ordnance Factories Board, and hence the name Jonga - Jabalpur Ordnance and Guncarriage Assembly. We don't know how he got hold of an Army vehicle.

He started roaming Hazratganj, Aminabad, Gomti Nagar and other major marketplaces in this open Jonga. The SSP was sure he would have returned to Lucknow. Earlier too, he had the information about his presence in Lucknow when we were keeping a watch on schools while he killed Upendra Vikram Singh and three others. We divided ourselves into different teams and would go looking for him in areas from where we got reports of him being seen.

We would keep an eye on people, especially for three young men together, because we knew the group only had three people now. Shriprakash generally sat in the driving seat. One person who had seen Shriprakash would be with each team for identification. We went around in plainclothes.

That evening, I and two commandos were returning from Polytechnic crossing towards Gomti barrage in a blue police

Gypsy when we decided midstream to take a round of Viraj Khand.

The Gypsy got into a petrol pump opposite the office of Project Corporation to turn towards the Khand. The headlights fell on an open Jonga. There were three men - one sitting in the front, the other on the back seat and the third man standing near the vehicle. The man for identification ducked and looked dumbfounded.

"What happened?" I asked him.

Meanwhile, the Jonga reversed without letting the pump staff take out the nozzle from the fuel tank and sped off with lightning speed.

"Shriprakash... Shriprakash *tha wo* (It was Shriprakash)," the man spluttered.

It was raining heavily. We got after the Jonga following the red taillight. Then it disappeared. The rain blurred the vision. After around fifty metres, the red taillight was switched off and we couldn't see where the vehicle went.

The other teams were called. We hunted all parts of Gomti Nagar through the night, but he had vanished into thin air. Gomti Nagar is a planned township and we easily moved around in the lanes and alleyways, looking for an open jeep. Covered vehicles were also checked, but it proved to be a fool's errand.

The next morning, we assembled in the office, crestfallen and disappointed that we came so close to catching him, yet he slipped out. Gyaan flew. Everyone started pointing out at the slips - if they had done this, if they had done that, if they had put barriers, if they had checked properly...

He had escaped, but one thing was certain - we were closing in.

Shriprakash had vacated the house from where we recovered the Gypsy and some documents. He had taken a new house where he parked the Jonga and the gang left for Nepal overnight in another car.

After three days, he started calling people for extortion. Businessmen. Politicians. And even the police this time.

People who paid him didn't tell the police but exerted pressure on the Vyapar Mandal. The Vyapar Mandal leaders would mount pressure on the police. Everyone would run us down in their choicest words; newspapers were ruthless in the opprobrium. It was difficult for us to face the officers and the public - we looked helpless against one man.

The Vyapar Mandal called for a bandh in Hazratganj under the leadership of Banwari Lal Kanchhal. The market was closed. There was a massive agitation. The DG was called. The SSP defended us. "See what all we have done. It's just one man and we are so close to him. The team is very competent and works round the clock. The pressure is demotivating and disturbing."

But the politicians, the public and the government are concerned with the results. It didn't matter to them that we had recovered the car used to kidnap Moolraj Arora, got one AK-47 and had killed one of the active gang members, who was no less dangerous than Shriprakash.

After the Hazratganj bandh, Shriprakash also got Kanchhal's kundali made. The leader got a call and he got so scared that he went to Mumbai for some days. The businessmen in Lucknow understood what may have happened.

Shriprakash was now calling people with double vigour.

Arun Kumar was a hard task master. "Follow all numbers that

people share with us, send teams. We will surely find something... *kuch to milega,*" he told us.

The numbers that businessmen were called from were all from Nepal. The Gorakhpur team was sent to Nepal to verify them. They went to all the PCOs, asking about people who made those calls, if they were the same set of people every time or different, the vehicles they used, and other descriptions about the people making those calls.

The team found one PCO where the caller had come three days in a row. The operator gave us the person's description and also provided some more numbers. Our team had the local police with us. The PCO operator told us that he could prepare a list of more numbers that were called. Within an hour, he handed a list to the team.

The next time Shriprakash went to the PCOs, the operator said, "Who do you call? The police came asking for you. There were local constables with them."

Shriprakash didn't stop even for a second and came straight to the hotel.

"Even the PCOs aren't safe," he told Sudhir and Anuj. "Four days ago, they chased us in Lucknow, and now they have landed at the PCOs."

This was a piece of very disturbing news for the gang. The police had managed to reach his house and seized the Gypsy; reached Mokama, seized an Ambassador and RK Singh's pistol. How could Shriprakash believe that someone from the gang was not being disloyal?!

"They cannot trace us through the mobile phones. We talk on the move. Between the beginnings of the calls to the end, I travel for at least twenty kilometres. Where will the police search for me in these twenty kilometres?"

Shriprakash sometimes thought Sudhir and Anuj were the moles. Because they would often say Anand shouldn't have been killed. They also thought that Shriprakash got him killed. When Shriprakash called the newspapers to tell them that anyone who betrays the gang gets killed, Sudhir and Anuj didn't like it.

It was decided to pack bags and leave Nepal right away. "We need to go to a place for making these calls that police will take at least two days to reach. They have come to Viratnagar and Kathmandu also," Shriprakash said. "And let's not stay at one place for more than a day."

Anuj and Sudhir didn't like this idea. "*Aise to police kabhi bhi, kahin bhi aa jayegi* (the police might come anytime anyway)," they said, sounding unsure about Shriprakash's suggestion. But Shriprakash was overbearing. He would silence them. They didn't have a choice.

Shriprakash was also shaken to the core by the development. On the one hand, he was claiming to be Lucknow's undisputed leader and, on the other, he was trying to run away from the police.

"We will not go to Lucknow or Gorakhpur, we will go to Bihar," Shriprakash suggested. They crossed the Raxual border and went to Araria.

It was six in the evening. They checked into a hotel and stayed the night. The next morning, Shriprakash called Surajbhan from a PCO. "Dada, for the past twenty days, strange things are happening with us. The police raided Mokama, they killed Anand, they chased me in Lucknow and now they came even to Nepal - these are ill omens," he said. "The government has formed teams that work all the time to chase me. Maybe someone from my team is helping the police."

Surajbhan calmed his nerves and said he shouldn't worry about the police in Bihar. Meanwhile, Surajbhan reminded him about a task he had given him for Araria.

"Yes, I remember, dada. That's why I have called you. I don't want the police to be coming behind me, I want to give them work."

Smuggling from Nepal was rampant in Uttar Pradesh, Bihar and West Bengal. Electronic items, gadgets, mobile phones, radio, transistors and televisions were smuggled into India from different borders. There was a man in Araria who was against Surajbhan's men or supporters engaged in this illegal business.

Shriprakash said he would call an hour later. "Send someone to identify the target," he said.

They drove down fifteen kilometres and called Surajbhan from a new PCO. He suspected that police may locate the first PCO. Anuj and Sudhir stood outside. He had a small chat and came out after the two signaled that there was no danger.

Surajbhan told him that a man in a red cap called Chandan would meet them outside a shoe store near Ghantaghar. "You don't go to him; he will come to you and tell your name. Take him with you. He will identify the target for you," Surajbhan instructed.

To be sure, the man was there. He came to Shriprakash's car and said, "Are you Ashok Singh bhaiyya?"

Shriprakash asked his name and told him to jump in. They went out of the Araria city area. There was a market complex where Chandan asked Shriprakash to slow down. A man was sitting on a chair on a raised platform. About twenty men surrounded him.

"The man sitting at the centre with kurta and *lungi*... he is the one," Chandan said.

Everyone carefully observed the man. They kept studying him from head to toe till the car turned and he went out of sight.

Chandan was dropped. The gang picked their weapons from the hotel, checked out and went on the mission. Shriprakash said they will leave Araria even if they failed to kill the target, because they had used three PCOs and someone may come sniffing after them.

Anuj drove the car; Shriprakash sat in the front with a pistol and Sudhir was in the back seat, holding the AK-47.

"We will stop only for ten seconds. After that don't stop for anything," Shriprakash told the team 100 metres before the market complex.

They came to the man. The window was rolled down. Sudhir emptied the AK-47 magazine on the man. Shriprakash fired at other people. There was a car facing in the direction the gang would flee. Someone was sitting in the driver's seat. Shriprakash killed him too.

After some time, Shriprakash asked Sudhir, "*Lag gayee thi na* (Did the bullets hit the man)?"

Sudhir said, "I am sure at least twenty bullets would have pierced the man's body. There was no chance of survival."

After they drove for about fifty kilometres, they stopped near a PCO. Shriprakash called Surajbhan. He told him that the mission had been accomplished and asked him where they should go.

"Go to Patna. I will make the arrangements."

"Not Patna, dada. It's not safe."

"Ok, then come to Mokama," Surajbhan said before disconnecting.

Chapter 13
Endgame

After the Araria murder, the gang decided to go to Delhi. Lucknow and Gorakhpur were unsafe - the police were hard on their heels. Sudhir was unsure about this decision.

"Our old friend Siriya Pahelwan is already dead. Where will we stay?" Sudhir asked irritatedly.

"We will find someone in his office who will recognise us and offer us help with the lodging."

"Can't we go to Gorakhpur first? From there, I am sure, someone can find out from Pahelwan's office if there are people capable of helping us in Delhi. Landing there directly without knowing about any local support may not be a good decision," Sudhir tried to reason with Shriprakash, but the gang leader was more worried about getting caught. The way the police had gone to the PCOs they used made him jittery.

During this discussion, Shriprakash suddenly remembered hearing the name STF. "What is this damn thing?" he asked. Sudhir and Anuj also didn't know anything about it, so they decided to use one of their men in Lucknow who prepared kundali to get more information on the STF.

"I will ask Rakesh Mani to find out about this. We need to know how this is different than the normal police teams," Sudhir said.

By the evening, the gang had full information about the STF from Rakesh.

"The STF is headed by Ajay Raj Sharma, whom the Chief Minister brought back as ADG LO to finish the gang. He has put together a team of officers who are known to be experts at solving organised crimes. Arun Kumar is the SSP of the STF. He's the police officer who brought down the dreaded Mukhtar Ansari by raiding his house in Ghazipur and defenestrating its belongings like flying saucers. Arun Kumar was the SP of the district. He clamped curfew before taking a heavy force to the house. The Ansaris – Mukhtar and Afzal – were formidable in eastern UP. Police didn't dare to serve the summons on them. The police attached the house in connection with a constable's murder. There's another story about Arun Kumar. During an election, Pappu Yadav was trying to enter UP from Bihar with more than a hundred vehicles. The police officer stopped the cavalcade at the border. Yadav's men tried to act smart; the officer ordered his men to tan their hide. Pappu Yadav now thinks twice before trying to pull off such an act. Then there's one Satyendra Vir Singh. He is from western UP and has been the SP City in Lucknow before getting into the STF. He has a good hold on criminals in the western parts of the state and has contacts in Delhi Police too. Rajesh Pandey is the officer who liaisons with mobile service providers for call details and is known to have developed a contraption to record mobile phone conversations," Rakesh blurted out all the information in one breath to Sudhir.

When Sudhir narrated this to Shriprakash, Shriprakash concluded that the reason that police had come so close to the gang in the recent past was because of the contraption device.

Sudhir told Shriprakash about other members of the special force as he listened intently.

"Huh! So they have been listening to our mobile phones," Shriprakash led out a sigh. "No wonder they always came behind us. I was under the impression that mobile phones cannot be tracked."

He ordered that the gang will not use mobile phones – or use it sparingly. "We will use it when it is absolutely necessary. And use multiple phones. Sudhir, look for someone who can get us many phone numbers. We will not use one number for even two calls. One phone, one call."

Shriprakash then asked Sudhir to also find out from the man, who had told him about police listening to their mobile phones, how to escape wiretapping.

He was thinking of how to prevent the police from reaching them as they tracked their mobile phones and Sudhir was relieved that they will now be beyond doubt. The gang realised that Shriprakash doubted their loyalty; he suspected one of them – Sudhir or Anuj – to be a mole.

Meanwhile, it was decided that they would use the mobile phone at least fifty kilometres away from where they were staying, and use it on the go so that the police find it difficult to track them down on the basis of mobile network.

These discussions were happening as their car crossed Varanasi, Allahabad and Kanpur and entered Delhi. They drove straight to Siriya Pahelwan's office. Most people there didn't know about this gang. But there was an old hand. He recognised Shriprakash and took him inside. Shriprakash said they needed shelter for a couple of days until they found a place to rent.

"Tell us a safe place for a few days. Then we will make our arrangements," he said.

The man obliged. At the temporary lodging, Shriprakash told Anuj to scan the newspapers for a house in a posh locality. Anuj had worked in East-West Airways and knew English. Shriprakash presumed that classified advertisements about houses in posh localities available on rent are carried in English dailies only. Anuj scoured the papers and called numbers mentioned in the classified ads. The idea behind renting a house in a posh locality was that police would seldom suspect that a criminal could have a hideout in such a place.

The search let them to a flat in Sector D of Vasant Kunj in South Delhi. It was on the first floor. The landlord was private secretary of a former prime minister. Police would think twice before raiding the house because they would be well aware about its owner. It suited the gang. It had a balcony from where they could keep a watch and give others a warning if there was danger. The staircase had a glass window through which they could escape if there was a raid or any other problem. They finalised it and decided to move into it soon.

Shriprakash reiterated that no one should talk on their mobile phones from the flat. "When we need to talk, we will go out, and be at a distance of at least twenty kilometres from the flat before we use our mobile phone," he said, "and no two calls from the same number."

Anuj got five new mobile phones and twelve SIM cards using a fake driving license. In those times, DL was the most used photo ID for taking mobile phone connections. In a bid to outdo their competitors, the operators were often not fussy about the IDs. They even kept some pre-activated SIMs for people who wanted one for immediate use. Otherwise, it took the mobile companies some time to activate the numbers.

After settling in the flat, they again started their hunt for money. Shriprakash was against using money parked in Mokama and said it was kept for a rainy day. The only way they could arrange money was through extortion or ransom.

For the lack of a readymade kundali, Shriprakash called Moolraj Arora. "You haven't paid the remaining money - you thought I will forget? Pay up, otherwise, I will pick you up again or your daughter," he said angrily.

Arora began pleading. He had actually believed that the trouble was over for him. He said he had paid what he could and now his business was in the doldrums. Then it struck him that the way to divert Shriprakash was to tell him about another wealthy man. He would focus on the new find and, at least for some more time, Arora would be off the hook.

He told Shriprakash about Aarif Builders. "He has many buildings in Lucknow. Also, he has hotels in Lucknow, Nainital and even in Dubai. He is well-heeled. You can make a killing," Arora said, before blurting out the businessman's telephone number.

The trick worked. Shriprakash calmed down. "Okay, I give you ten days. If he doesn't fall in line, be ready with the money," he said.

Arora wanted to get out of this and replied meekly, "Okay."

Shriprakash called several other people. He was desperate for money. But he was smarter - he called different people from different numbers and different locations. Some calls were made from Noida, some from Gurgaon. He used different locations in and around Delhi. We were tracking the numbers, so it was decided to have a team permanently perched in Delhi. Satyendra Vir Singh was tasked with gathering information about the possible hideouts of Shriprakash in Delhi. He was to use his contacts in the Delhi Police for this task.

It had been three months to the formation of the STF and we hadn't delivered the result that the government wanted. The force was formed for six months only, and half of that time was over. The officers were also worried about different rumours doing the rounds - one of them was that Shriprakash had fled to Thailand. Suppose it took us more than six months to reach him, shouldn't we also focus on some other criminals carrying rewards? After all, that was also the STF's mandate. So it was decided to widen our net and look for other big fish in the crime world.

Meanwhile, Shriprakash called Aarif Builders. Aarif thought it was a hoax and hung up. The call came again. "This will cost you dearly. If you don't listen to me, you will be killed like others. I am Ashok Singh," the caller said.

Aarif shared this with his friends and relatives. People told him that Shriprakash was a big criminal. Aarif thought someone was using the gangster's name to threaten him so he tapped his phone to record the next call to his house in the cantonment.

Then he told one of his doctor friends. The doctor knew ADG LO Ajay Raj Sharma. He called the police officer and sought an appointment. It was late in the evening; the ADG told him to come the next morning but the doctor insisted it was urgent and needed an immediate hearing. The ADG agreed to meet the doctor.

Aarif told the ADG everything. He told him that Shriprakash wanted ₹50,000 for every flat that Aarif Builders were making in their new projects in Paper Mill Colony. Ajay Raj Sharma said he will ask an officer from the STF to confirm if the voice in the recording was that of Shriprakash. Aarif was also told to engage the caller in a long conversation the next time he called. "The longer you engage him, the easier it will be for us to locate him," the man was told.

But Aarif was terrorised and he said he won't dare to take the next call.

The next morning, Arun Kumar asked me to go to Aarif's house to listen to the tape. "If it is him, it will be easier for us to track him down while the call is on. You never know, we may get his live location with the help of the Delhi Police," he said before sending me off.

I was at the cantonment house with my team. The tape was placed in the player and no sooner did it start playing than I declared it was indeed Shriprakash. The ADG LO and STF SSP were informed about this. Aarif began perspiring when he learnt that he was on the radar of such a dreadful criminal.

We wanted to engage Shriprakash in a conversation when he called next, but Aarif had thrown in the towel. We decided to look for someone who could impersonate Aarif, someone who was soft-spoken and used a mix of Urdu in speech.

We realised that one head constable in our team, Fazrullah, could fit the bill. He was asked to stay at Aarif's and practise talking like him. The telephone exchange was requested to alert us when there was a call on Aarif's number.

The call came and our head constable answered. They spoke for nearly twenty minutes. This was insufficient for live tracking, but we knew the call originated from Delhi. The good news was Shriprakash couldn't get a hint that he was talking to an impersonator.

When Shriprakash called the second time, Fazrullah was more confident.

"Hello."

"Did you arrange the money?" Shriprakash asked urgently. It was unlikely of him to let the other person know his desperation. But time was ticking for him.

"I haven't kept track of the finance. Give me time to consult my accountant to find out how much he can take out from the project budget."

Shriprakash bought the logic. "I will call after a day."

The two calls were tracked to two different locations – both around Delhi. There was no static location. Meanwhile, Fazrullah was prepped for the third call. "Sound petrified, buoy him up, tell him that you are aware of his power," the head constable was told. This, we felt, may help lengthen the conversation. If the number or location is repeated, we may catch him during the call itself.

When Shriprakash called after a day, Fazrullah said he knew what would happen to him if he failed to pay, but it was difficult to give him so much money at once. "There are project managers and chartered accountants and I may not be able to siphon so much money out. Plus, the police will be after my life when they find out that I paid," he said, gauging intently Shriprakash's mood.

He was calm. "When you know everything," he said, "then why delay?"

"I need time to mop up the amount."

"How much time?" asked the mollified gangster.

"At least a week."

Shriprakash agreed. "I will call after a week," he said. "Keep the money ready. You will have to deliver it to where I tell you."

Fazrullah sounded as if he had kittens. "Me?" he asked. "But I won't have the heart."

Shriprakash agreed to this one too. He was really appeased by his praise. "Okay," he said, "keep the money ready. I will send someone to collect it."

During his stay in Delhi, Shriprakash had got interested in English newspapers. Anuj would brief him about what they were writing about the gang. "Hindi newspapers are parochial; English newspapers will make you a national criminal. People in Delhi read the English papers," Anuj told him. "For the political agenda, it was important that the English newspapers also write lucidly about our reign of terror."

Before this, Shriprakash would find out every morning about what the newspapers in Gorakhpur and Lucknow had written about him. After Anuj's counsel, he began calling up crime reporters of English newspapers too.

One day, when he called a contact in Gorakhpur to share the news about him, he was told that police had taken his brother, Omprakash, and his family to Cantonment Police Station. "There are reports that the police have tortured them," the man said.

Shriprakash felt exasperated and dialled Gorakhpur SSP. "You want bloodbath at Gol Ghar?" he asked angrily. Before the SSP could say anything, the gangster continued, "I will come and kill twenty people there and you will be suspended. How did the police dare to touch the women of my family? Release them immediately," he boomed.

"It's not in my hands," the SSP said. "The STF came and took them to the police station. I'm sure you've heard of the STF that the CM has formed. Only they can release them."

Shriprakash looked more flustered on hearing this. He called the DGP.

"I am Amarmani Tripathi. Let me talk to the DGP," he said.

The line was connected and the DGP answered.

"How dare you touch the women of my family?" he thundered.

Aghast, the DGP asked, "Who's this?"

"Shriprakash."

"How dare you call me?"

"*Ghar walon ko thane par baithane ki himmat kaise hui* (How dare you to drag my family members to the police station)?" Shriprakash said seething with rage. "I know how to put pressure on you people. I will come and fire so many bullets in Hazratganj that you won't stay the DGP. That's the language you understand. Your CM will suspend you..."

The DGP had already disconnected. He called the ADG LO to his chamber and told him about Shriprakash's audacity. "How come he has the nerve to call me?"

The ADG LO said the families had been picked up as an old police practice – when snakes hide in holes, crush the snakelets and the snakes will come rushing out. The families, he said, were aware of everything. They benefit from the criminal acts. They get tenders in their names.

Everyone knew Shriprakash was impetuous, but how could he threaten the DGP?! Security around the DGP office was ramped up. The newspapers got alarmed by the security beef-up, but didn't know the reason. Different newspapers guessed different reasons.

Shriprakash thought the police would be spooked by his calls and release his family. He was wrong – the calls didn't have any impact.

The gangster then called three ministers who lived in Gorakhpur. He told, almost ordered, them to get his family released. Otherwise, he threatened, they will all face the music. "If you want me to spill your blood, so be it," he said.

The ministers got worried. They talked to each other and decided to meet the CM for this because it was only he who could tell the STF to release the family members.

An appointment was taken. The CM could figure out why three senior ministers of his cabinet wanted to see him so urgently. When the appointment was given, two other ministers, who hadn't been able to meet the CM for a long time, also tagged along.

When they met Kalyan Singh, the senior-most among them spoke. "Police are harassing the family of Shriprakash. It's sending a wrong message."

"Wrong message?" the CM interposed. "What do you want? That we should let the families enjoy the perks and Shriprakash can go on unleashing terror? I am surprised that five ministers have come here to plead for a monster," the CM was extremely curt. He signalled them to leave.

Outside the CM's house, the three discussed among

themselves what they will tell Shriprakash when he would call in the evening. They decided that they will tell him that the meeting didn't happen because of the CM's engagements. They will put it off for tomorrow, they thought.

He did call and the ministers dished out the decided line.

On the other hand, the CM called the DGP after the ministers left. "There's no need to go soft on them. Send them to jail, and pick families of other gang members also." The CM's order was terse.

The family was sent to jail. When Shriprakash heard about it, he felt confused. "But the ministers said they will meet the CM and sort it out," he wondered to the person who provided the information.

"They are liars, bhaiya – they met the CM and were scoffed. The secretary of the health minister is from Gorakhpur. He told me that his minister was in a foul mood after returning from the CM's office. Looks like the CM didn't treat him too well."

It was later learnt that the two ministers, who tagged along for want of an appointment, went back and apologised to the CM. They said they came with the three because they hadn't got an appointment for some time.

Shriprakash dialled the ministers and spewed venom on them. "I know how the CM packed you off. You are good for nothing," he said. "Let me handle this myself. If they want to suffer, let them suffer."

He banged the phone down indignantly.

Meanwhile, the police picked up the families of Anuj and Sudhir too. Everyone was booked for sheltering criminals and sent to jail.

In the Vasant Kunj flat, the three felt piqued that their families were suffering because of them. Shriprakash said he knew how to handle the CM. "I think I need to do something big now," he muttered under his breath and the other two looked curiously at him.

Then Anuj spoke. "Sometimes," he said, "we despise the little ones. Rahim said, '*Jahan kaam aawe sui, kaha kare talwari* (where a needle is good enough, what use is a sword)?' Just wring the neck of an inspector and it will be sorted."

Shriprakash called the inspector of Cantonment Police Station. The inspector literally started crying. "Don't blame me, bhaiyya," he said, "I am in a piquant situation – if I don't listen to you, someone will come and kill me; if I don't listen to the STF, I will get suspended."

Shriprakash wasn't interested in him anymore. He disconnected. "*Sipahi daroga kuch nahi kar sakte* (Minions can't help us). We need to get either an STF officer or the CM," he said. "There's a lot of security around the CM so he may be difficult, but we can go for someone close to him. This is getting us a bad name in Gorakhpur. By the way," he suddenly remembered, "we need to call Aarif."

When they went out to call Aarif, they incidentally went to the same place from where Shriprakash had made a call a few days ago. The police were already there. It was a small market and the police were talking to the people. Shriprakash thought they may be over thinking and sent Anuj to check.

He went and noticed that UP Police was asking for the address of the mobile phone tower. He beat a hasty retreat. "*Wahi hain.*

Tower ka address pooch rahe hain (It's them. The policeman was asking for the address of the mobile tower)," he said.

Shriprakash looked incredulous. "What's a tower got to do with us?"

Anuj explained to him that the locations of mobile phones are traced through the towers.

"I don't believe this," Shriprakash said and suggested they go to a spot near Mayur Vihar where they had gone the previous day.

They went there, got down, bought cold drinks, and were casually roaming the market where they asked one of the shop-keepers who had a mobile tower atop his establishment, "How did you get this tower?"

The shopkeeper got alarmed. "Why is everyone asking about mobile towers today?" he asked. "Some people came in the morning, also asking for the tower."

It didn't take much time for Shriprakash to realise that the UP Police had been there. They got back into the car and sped off.

Shriprakash used to speak to a tantric guru in Calcutta whenever he was in distress. They went to a new location and he called "Guruji". "Bad times have befallen us, Guruji," he said, "police are closing in on us." He told him the events of the past few days in detail.

Guruji asked him how many skulls Goddess Kali carried around her neck. He didn't know.

"Hundred and one," Guruji said. "That's what makes her invincible. Do you get me? Become invincible."

Shriprakash didn't keep a count of people he had killed, but he had a faint idea that he had touched that magical number.

"Now I got it," he said to Sudhir and Anuj. "We need to complete killing hundred and one people to get out of trouble."

They decided to come back to the flat and do the math. Back in Vasant Kunj, Shriprakash said they needed to instill fear even in the CM. He was shaken to the core by the police brutality on his family and the fact that the police had come to places from where he had made calls.

Shriprakash learnt that the son of a slain BJP leader wanted to get in touch with him. Sudhir and Anuj were against this. This, they said, was not the right time to meet anyone. "For all we know, he may be a plant," they said. Shriprakash said he won't meet him but there was no harm in giving him a call.

The son of the leader said he wanted Shriprakash's help in avenging his father's murder.

Shriprakash had narrowed down on a sadhu from Farukkhabad who had an ashram in Delhi. "He is close to the CM. If we can get to him, we can intimidate the CM and he will be forced to release our families," Shriprakash said.

Sudhir and Anuj felt it was too risky a proposition and didn't come on board immediately, but they were always hemmed in eventually.

The gang decided to do a recce of the ashram. They went there, surveyed the area, and looked at the entry and exit points and the place from where the sadhu delivered his sermons. But there was a problem. It was September and a blanket would look out of place. They may have to wait for another month – the end of October or early November – to carry out the mission.

Shriprakash was fiercely wayward and desperate for a big bang. Something that would shake the state's top political leadership. Something that would keep his terror alive.

They went there again the next day. All entries were closed. The security told them that the sadhu had gone out of Delhi and won't be back in a week.

Shriprakash felt disappointed and returned to the flat. The name of Aarif came to his mind again. When he called the builder, we noticed that some numbers had been called before the call to Aarif. Two of those numbers were landlines from Gorakhpur.

Arun Kumar requested DIG SN Singh for putting those numbers on surveillance. But he stressed that this shouldn't get out. "They may get alarmed and stop calling these numbers," he said, "which will make it difficult for the STF to track them down." The DIG assured our SSP that he had set up the recording facility at his residence and that he dealt with the telephone exchange for surveillance directly, so there was no way anyone could find out about the activity.

Shriprakash called Aarif again. Fazrullah wasn't around and Aarif didn't have the guts to receive the call. He asked one of his servants to answer the call. Shriprakash asked for Aarif and was told that he wasn't home. When the servant asked the caller to identify himself, he said, "Tell him that Ashok Singh called."

This call too had come from Delhi.

It was decided that we must go to Delhi now because we had traced his location to Delhi and nearby places for the last couple of days. All of us were fed up with the bad press and it seemed that this was the best time to nab him and silence our detractors.

We landed in Delhi on 19 September 1998. PP Singh, the Delhi Police inspector, put us up in a hotel near the Azadpur Mandi. We asked the crime branch colleagues there about how we could record mobile phones. We had been hearing the conversations but hadn't been able to record them.

In the mid-1990s, operators were ill-equipped to intercept calls. Today, every cellular service provider has an aggregation station which is a clutch of servers called mediation servers (because they mediate between the cellular operators and the law enforcement agencies) to intercept phones.

The Delhi crime branch said they had created a little contraption attached to a tape recorder. We needed old, unused phones for this. Luckily, there were two Sony Ericsson phones with us which had become dysfunctional. The crime branch helped us get the recording system working with the help of these two phones. We would be recording mobile phone conversations for the first time; until then, we had recorded landline calls and listened to mobile phones.

The SSP sent a request letter to the Delhi Police for putting the numbers on surveillance. "He is our most wanted and we need to listen to the conversions on these numbers," he wrote. Shriprakash was using five mobile numbers. We needed to listen to all of them and record the calls.

We heard a call go to the airport in the evening. The caller said he had missed the morning flight to Ranchi and wanted to know if the dates of the three tickets could be shifted for the day after. The man at the inquiry said there was no provision. "Please come to the counter and check. If someone travelled in your place, there may be a chance," the airline staff said.

Anuj said he had worked for an airline that allowed this kind of adjustment, but the man didn't seem to budge an inch. "Come to the counter, sir. Let me consult with my seniors in the meanwhile."

I told the team about this call. Arun Kumar spoke to the DCP Airport Security and requested him to alert us if someone came to transfer three tickets to Ranchi. "We need to detain him," he said.

The next day, we went to the airport at around 9 a.m. We were there for a long time, but no one came. We returned. In the evening, there was another call that made my ears prick up. Shriprakash answered the call from Surajbhan.

The Bihar man asked the gangster if his man came. "Yes, he came," Shriprakash said. "We have sent him with the weapons by road; we will take the morning flight on the 23rd. Please get us picked from the airport."

So, they were planning an operation in Ranchi. Probably, they booked new tickets without visiting the airport. And they would be without weapons at the airport – a good opportunity for us to catch them.

The SSP spoke to the DCP again. "He's UP's most wanted. Let us arrest him," he said, but the DCP said it couldn't be allowed.

"We will arrest him, produce him before a magistrate and you can seek transit remand," the DCP said.

That won't be right, we thought. There was no guarantee that the magistrate will give us the remand. So we decided to nab the gang before it entered the airport.

"Let's go there around four in the morning," the SSP said detailing the plan. "We will check vehicles at all the entry points to the airport area. We will request the Delhi Police to set up an additional barrier before the airport barrier. We know the vehicle he's using. When we spot it, we will drag him out and pin him down - there's no way he can escape us this time."

Meanwhile, in Lucknow, one of our officers was coordinating with Fazrullah and the Gorakhpur DIG for new calls from Shriprakash. A call went to Aarif Builders. It was from a landline in Greater Kailash. The Delhi Police crime branch informed us that the call was made from a PCO.

A little later, we were informed that Shriprakash was talking to the Gorakhpur landline from the same PCO in Greater Kailash.

We had to rush to the PCO while the call was on. Greater Kailash was around forty kilometres away from where we were putting up. We would get him at the airport the next day, but we needed to confirm and see for ourselves how he looked. There were several rumours about that in Lucknow. Some said that Shriprakash has grown a beard while others were sure that he had got a plastic surgery done from Bangkok and we wouldn't recognise the new face. So it was important to find out his new look before we swooped down on him at the airport, we thought. The PCO operator would tell us what vehicle he was using apart from describing his looks. After the visit to the PCO, we thought we would go to the airport for the final plan.

The PCO was in a very posh locality and the operator was a South Indian.

He said, "The man made a long STD call." He retrieved the numbers for us when we told him that we were from the UP Police. He continued, "The three men came in a blue Cielo. Two went inside and one was waiting outside. They were here just now, wouldn't have gone far. You may catch them at the red light," he said.

We rushed out without letting him dish out anything more and hit the road. Soon, the blue Cielo was spotted in the traffic. We started following it. The car reached Ghaziabad border. Arun Kumar alerted VPN Singh, an inspector posted in Ghaziabad, to track the car if it went beyond our sight. Singh had earlier worked in Arun Kumar's team when the officer was posted as SSP of Ghaziabad.

He called to report that the car was headed towards Indirapuram. "I have alerted police outposts there. They are setting up barricades; it can't get out of here now because Indirapuram is underdeveloped and the roads are bad," he told the SSP. Cielo was a distinct car and very few people had it back then. It was a very luxurious car and easy to spot in traffic. People kept telling us about it on the way.

Around 11.30 a.m., we spotted it near a police barrier. There was an adrenaline rush in all of us – this was the moment for which we had been waiting. Here he was – in front of us. The Cielo reversed on seeing the barricade and turned on to what looked like a dirt track, but there was no road there and the car got stuck after hitting an American babool.

We parked our Tata Sumo to block the road and with the AK-47s, got off to walk towards the Cielo.

Ratatatatatatatata...Firing started. We retaliated with fire. The three got off the car and began running. VPN Singh had also rushed in with his team. People from the ill-developed colonies around the spot gathered at the spot.

The firing stopped. The three men were on the ground. We waited before we could go near them – they could fire again, we thought. Some more shots were fired, and when we noticed no action, we went closer.

The three were lying on the ground, soaked in blood. The game had finally ended. The blood of so many officers was avenged. The man who rose to infamy in a short span of five years lived by the gun and eventually died by the gun. Shriprakash's reign of terror ended.

Epilogue

Shripprakash's end was the result of fourteen months of hard work. The man carried a reward of two lakh rupees on his arrest; the aides, Anand Pandey, Sudhir Tripathi and Anuj Pratap Singh, also had rewards on their arrests.

After confirming their death, the bodies were searched. Some diaries and weapons were recovered. Some mobile phones were also recovered. We dialled our numbers from them to verify that these were the same numbers that were being tapped.

Arun Kumar called the DGP from the spot. The police chief passed the information to the principal secretary (Home). It was 22 September 1998 and a special budget session of the Assembly was on. The CM was presenting the budget. PS (Home) scrawled something on a small chit and called the marshal to take it to the CM.

Kalyan Singh looked at the slip and paused. His face lit up. He glanced up from the budget speech and looking at the Speaker, said, "*Adyaksha mahoday*, please allow me to make a very important announcement." Kesari Nath Tripathi, who was the Speaker, allowed it.

"Shriprakash and his two aides died in an encounter with the STF in Ghaziabad," the CM announced, rubbing his hands in glee.

The House rose with thunderous applause. The clapping continued as some ministers rushed in to congratulate the CM. So many of them must have heaved a sigh of relief, and some must have also felt bad.

In Ghaziabad, the local police had arrived for the legal formalities. The bodies were sealed and packed off to mortuary. A phalanx of police vehicles with red and blue lights descended; a battery of journalists from Delhi and Ghaziabad also arrived. Some TV crews thrust bulbous mikes in the face of SSP Ghaziabad, thinking it was a local police operation.

We were directed to reach Lucknow by the next flight. The DGP was to hold a press conference to announce the operation, we were told. So no one spoke to the media in Ghaziabad.

As we were getting ready to return to the hotel to pack our bags and rush to the airport, Arun Kumar got a call from Rajiv Ratan Shah, the former principal secretary (Home). It was due to his and the efforts of Ajay Raj Sharma that the STF was formed. Most of Shriprakash's horrifying crimes had occurred during his tenure.

"My wife and I want to see how that demon looked," said the officer, who was then posted in the Prasar Bharti. KK Rastogi's wife was a friend of Shah's wife. So there was a personal interest too. The bodies were in the mortuary and SSP Ghaziabad facilitated that the Shah couple was taken there.

We took the Delhi-Lucknow-Guwahati Indian Airlines flight, which got delayed due to inclement weather and a technical snag for nearly four hours. The aircraft touched down at the airport at around 10 p.m. Two prominent politicians emerged on the step-ladder ahead of us and were initially a little pleased to find people thronging the tarmac with bouquets and garlands at that odd hour. But their joy was short-lived as the people carrying flowers avoided them and rushed towards us.

The tarmac glazed in that poignant moment when we got off the flight. We preferred to stroll along the tarmac stretch to the airport lounge. Arun Kumar was mobbed by the media. He narrated the sequence of events to them at the VVIP lounge.

When we came out of the airport, around five thousand people were waiting for us. Lucknow SSP Rajni Kant Mishra, the full police force of district, full rank and file, all additional SPs, deputy SPs, inspectors, everyone was there. There was a police band and some other bands too. We were showered with petals and a PAC band party played the victory tune.

We were overwhelmed by the grand welcome.

Our families were also there to welcome us. We could imagine their happiness – they had spent sleepless nights with us as we racked our brains on browsing through the numbers and solidifying information. Our kids had stopped going to school. There were commandos at our houses.

Earlier, we had called our families from Ghaziabad after the shootout. They could have got alarmed on seeing breaking news on TV stations, so we wanted to give them the information ourselves. The wives disbelieved but when they called each other, they planned to come to the airport.

The STF team meandered towards the city in a convoy of cars escorted by Chetak patrol cars.

The Chief Minister announced in the House a cash prize of one lakh to each of the STF team members and an out-of-turn promotion. Gallantry promotions don't apply to gazette officers, so the government expedited our regular promotions.

Reena was a journalist with a reputed newspaper in Lucknow. She had been following the developments of the Shriprakash case from the beginning. She had received threatening calls from Shriprakash when she had downplayed Shriprakash's role in a murder case. She was personally invested in the case and knew about the tactics and plans of the police in and out.

The next day, there was a ceremony at Raj Bhawan. The Governor felicitated the STF and presented its members with saplings along with the cheque of award money. It was a moment of immense pride for the STF. Reena was also present at the ceremony and was quite happy. Now, finally, she could concentrate on something else apart from Shriprakash Shukla.

After the ceremony, when we went to the STF office, there were hundreds of people waiting for us. They were the people who had been harassed by Shriprakash – those who had reported to the police and also those who didn't dare to inform the police. Reena followed the team.

The principal of Karamat, Saima Khalid, was also there. She came with some teachers. "I may have mistreated you, sir, please forgive us," she said apologetically. Some more school principals came to thank the STF. The man who had become the most feared hitman after the sensational killings and kidnappings for huge ransom was dead. Obviously, they must have found out that the STF was trying to prevent kidnapping from their schools.

Reena dived forward to get an interview with Arun Kumar.

"Congratulations, sir! This is a huge achievement. I just have one question."

"Please go ahead," responded Arun Kumar cheerfully.

"Sir, we know that Shukla was suspecting a mole to be present in his gang. Was there any?"

Arun Kumar was a little taken aback at this question. He thought at that point, everyone would only be interested in how they managed to get the gangster killed. "No. He had finally figured out that we got to know about his locations from his mobile phone calls."

"That's very well, sir. But I believe he had many numbers and didn't use the same number for a long time."

"That's right!"

"Sir, mobile phones and numbers are easily procured with forged documents. How did you exactly find out which numbers the gang was using?" She was holding her breath for the revelation.

Arun Kumar paused for a moment, turned towards her and smiled. "You are someday going to be an excellent investigative journalist. I am sure you will yourself be able to find the answer to your question."

The crowd kept cheering as Arun Kumar and the rest of the STF stood with pride written all over their faces.

List of Acronyms

ADG	-	Additional Director General
CBI	-	Central Bureau of Investigation
DG	-	Director General
GRP	-	Government Railway Police
IGIMS	-	Indira Gandhi Institute of Medical Sciences
RA	-	Rural Area
RPF	-	Railway Protection Force
SOG	-	Special Operations Groups
SP	-	Superintendent of Police
STF	-	SPECIAL TASK FORCE

About the authors

Rajesh Pandey

IPS officer Rajesh Pandey retired as IG of Bareilly Range in Uttar Pradesh in May 2022. Currently, he is the nodal officer of the Uttar Pradesh Expressways Industrial Development Authority (UPEIDA), a government agency responsible for development of expressways in the state.

A native of Allahabad (now Prayagraj), Rajesh Pandey did Master's in Botany in 1982 from Allahabad University. He joined the Uttar Pradesh state police service as a deputy superintendent of police.

He was among the founding members of the elite UP STF (Special Task Force) when it was set up to deal with organised crime in 1998 and the Anti-Terrorism Squad (ATS) in 2009 for anti-terror operations. He headed the electronic surveillance during Shriprakash operation and is credited with putting together the first surveillance unit for police.

He has been part of 70 police encounters so far. He has investigated major terrorist attacks in the state of U.P. He has been awarded the Indian Police Medals for Gallantry four times -in 1999, 2000, 2007 and 2016 - for Operation Bazooka, and for successfully interrogating the Faizabad and Varanasi terror attacks. Pandey went to the United Nations Peace Keeping Mission in Kosovo in 2008 and won the United Nations Medal for Peace Keeping.

After being inducted into the Indian Police Service (Batch of 2003 SPS), he was posted as Superintendent of Police at Rae

Bareli and Gonda, and as SSP at Saharanpur, Lucknow, Aligarh and Meerut.Subsequently, he was posted on the post of Deputy Inspector General of Police (Security) in Uttar Pradesh.

He is fond of narrating stories from his police career on his YouTube channel (https://www.youtube.com/c/IPSRajeshPandey), which he started during the Covid-19 lockdown.

Rakesh Goswami

Rakesh Goswami is a professor at the Indian Institute of Mass Communication, New Delhi, and is in charge of admissions, examinations and short courses. Prior to this appointment, he has been the regional director of IIMC's Northern Regional Centre at Jammu. He has been a journalist for 20 years, working across the electronic and print media before taking the plunge into academics. He began his career from *Hindustan Times* Lucknow as a sub editor and graduated to reporting, handling the medical and health beat.

He has worked with Channel 7 (later rechristened as IBN7 and now called Network18India), as the Rajasthan bureau chief in Jaipur. He returned to the print, his first love, after being in the television news industry for nine years, and headed the editorial operations of *Hindustan Times* in Rajasthan.

Goswami has always been fascinated by crime reporting and would often tag along the crime reporter to the office of Rajesh Pandey, then SP City in Lucknow. He has known Pandey since then. During the Covid-19 lockdown, when Pandey decided to write the true story of the rise and fall of one of UP's most dreaded gangsters, he collaborated with Goswami.

Goswami did his Bachelor's in Science (Statistics and Computer Science) from Lucknow University and started working soon after graduating. Son of a clerk, Goswami freelanced for *The Pioneer*, *The Times of India* and *Hindustan Times* in Lucknow during college to earn his pocket money.

A University Gold Medalist in Master's in Journalism, Goswami chose Rajasthan films for his doctoral thesis.